ISAAC
a modern fable

Also by Ivan G. Goldman

FICTION

Where the Money Is: A Novel of Las Vegas

The Barfighter

Exit Blue

NON-FICTION

L.A. Secret Police (with Mike Rothmiller)

IVAN G. GOLDMAN

ISAAC

a modern fable

The Permanent Press
Sag Harbor, NY 11963

For information, address:
  The Permanent Press
  4170 Noyac Road
  Sag Harbor, NY 11963
  www.thepermanentpress.com

Library of Congress Cataloging-in-Publication Data

Goldman, Ivan G.—
    Isaac : a modern fable / Ivan G. Goldman.
        p. cm.
        I. Title.

PS3557.O3686I83 2012
813'.54—dc23   2011050141

Printed in the United States of America.

In memory of my cousin Tech 4 Marvin N. Gillman,
509th Parachute Infantry Battalion, 1924–1944,
and my uncle Yankl Balaban, Russian soldier,
who died at Stalingrad, *c.* 1942

I am with you, you men and women of a generation, or
  ever so many generations hence,
Just as you feel when you look on the river and sky, so I felt.

— WALT WHITMAN
   "Crossing Brooklyn Ferry"

And flesh itself is magic
Dancing on a clock,
And time itself
The magic length of God.

— LEONARD COHEN
   "God Is Alive, Magic Is Afoot"

CHAPTER 1

RUTH

Rick, as it turned out, wore jumbo wristbands with shiny metal studs, Teutonic black boots, and a watch chain that could double as a ship's anchor. The accessories probably proclaimed his allegiance to some renegade sub-cult, but I was stuck without a codebook. He was a good seven or eight years older than the emailed photo that showed him poised to shoot a basketball, intent, good-humored, and full of life. His current body and head showed a balloon-y thickness that seasons had added like tree rings. The photo wasn't exactly a lie, but it wasn't true either, and as I approached his table it occurred to me that his deception was so obvious and pathetic it cried out for my compassion. He hadn't spotted me yet, and he was downcast and fidgeting, making little movements that advertised discomfort. I wondered whether the carefree Rick captured by the camera lived only in that lucky moment. Or perhaps he'd led a lovely life before it washed out from under him and he became the version of Rick before me now.

Of course I understood these judgments were based on bits of information that are generally deemed superficial. Yet the barbed wire tattoo that encircled an upper arm (one of the previous decade's fashion calamities) could easily be a more accurate mode of communication than actual conversation, which isn't always what it's cracked up to be. So many people out there can, for limited intervals, hide sullenness, viciousness, and a whole range of other deal-breaking and potentially unlawful characteristics, whereas a hairstyle or mode of dress broadcasts how a person wishes, at least, to be perceived.

By the time I reached Ground Zero I'd ferreted out so many little misrepresentations, wacky allegiances, and neurotic behaviors that I was seized by an urge to keep walking and skip further pain for both of us. A quick, dirty exit rather than the standard death by a thousand cuts. He hasn't looked up yet, and even if he had, so what? Snatch the moment, I screamed at myself (silent scream, of course).

Instead I stopped and introduced myself, trying to be simultaneously pleasant and businesslike as I pretended there was no swindle. Was it possible he detected the nature of the debate that had just raged between my ears? He jerked to his feet for a handshake and sat back down, legs crossed, jiggling one boot, and watching me carefully. Sinking into the chair across from him felt like going in for a root canal. I'd already scrubbed the original mission. Forget about finding prince charming and begin establishing a plausible defense for Evelyn's post-disaster criticism. *You gave up how soon?* Running off in less than thirty minutes might damage him more than the pass-by I should have executed in the first place. But who'd established these rules anyway? Probably the same martinets who told us to drink eight glasses of water a day and insure our cell phones.

"Excuse me," I said, glancing down at my cell phone as though screening a call from the secretary of commerce. Actually I was checking the time—a little past two; digital seconds swam through molasses.

His eyes kept straying to the little tortoise tattoo that peeked out from beneath a shoulder. Unless they were on my breasts, another unacceptable possibility. I checked myself out again. Simple white scooped jersey without too much scoop. I could wear the same outfit to church—well, some churches anyway. He poured me coffee from a pitcher already on the table. I found this only borderline thoughtful and potentially aggressive. What if I preferred tea or decaf? At this point I could have used a double vodka.

He'd come straight from a recording session and was disappointed I'd never heard of the musicians. Very quickly he began dropping other names, reciting his vast connections within the music business and describing the worldwide respect he'd earned thanks to his trendsetting acumen. I wondered how carefully this monologue had been composed beforehand and wished his efforts could be directed at someone who'd find a way to love him and make him relax.

It didn't take long to discover that Rick was apparently powerless to take his conversation from A to Z without stopping at every letter in between. As he described some alternative rock group he'd discovered somewhere, he had to name every step in the process—how he came to be in that particular little club, how he rated the place and why. He was mostly too loud, but the words faded into a mumble at the end of his sentences. Trying to make them out in a crowded food court buzzing with conversation was like being forced to work on an annoying puzzle.

Excluding criminal violence there are two kinds of disaster dates. Not standard mediocre dates. Downright disasters. First, there are the interrogators who turn what's supposed to be polite social discourse into a trip to the station house. Second, the narcissists too self-absorbed to ask any questions at all. It was clear which one I'd stumbled upon here. But then I remembered his emails, which, though not absolutely compelling, seemed to come from a decent, self-effacing soul. "I couldn't get through *Pride and Prejudice*," he wrote. "Now you confess something." Maybe a Cyrano wrote it for him. Or maybe he was a Jekyll and Hyde, and lucky me, Jekyll had the day off. Was it still possible to chase the terror out of him with kindness and forbearance and allow Dr. Jekyll to flower? Or was there no strategy to help him find his way back to the serenity he felt when his mother nursed him? Getting the hell out of there was more practical, and definitely more appealing. Meanwhile, compelled by nerves, he just kept wading deeper into his pit of self-created sludge. Why did the courtship ritual have to be so damn painful anyway? Was it really so crucial for males and females to find each other? What are we? Plumbing parts?

LENNY

I was trying to pick up the conversation of the young woman with the soft, lovely ponytail swinging behind her delicate ears toward an even lovelier ass, the one who'd swept past me to join her friend in the angry young man costume. What struck me was the way she moved, effortlessly like a cat, as though she weighed nothing at all. Our eyes locked for a millisecond and I looked away, making her think that I—who'd fought in countless wars, repelled bandits, pashas, punks from the Khyber Pass to Patagonia, survived thirst, starvation and untold encounters with idle cruelty—feared a pretty woman with an ironic smile. I did.

Her marriage finger was blissfully naked, but for all I knew she was living with wrath-man and they were meeting up to shop for new furniture. What's this? An aloof young mother with two small children sat down next to her, and I spotted confusion, then concern. What was going on over there?

RUTH

As I mapped out my getaway I noticed a sexy, curly-haired young man—younger than I was, I decided—observing our pathetic drama from a nearby table. I wondered whether he'd picked up enough of the conversation to know he was witnessing a lonely-hearts Internet meet-up. When I caught him watching he flashed a smile with his pleasant face and looked away, embarrassed. I liked him for that. He was compact, not ferociously handsome, but arresting, with a slight hook in his nose and big, black, expressive eyes. His sleeves were partially rolled up, and I noticed scars on the sinewy forearms plus a few smaller ones on his face and neck. They didn't seem to match, indicating he'd accumulated them on separate occasions and in different ways—burns, cuts, who knows? They spiced his aura with deeds and mystery. Lying on the sofa watching TV, you don't acquire scars.

The young, pretty Hispanic woman at the counter definitely noticed him too. She'd personally delivered his bagel and coffee, earning herself an amused shake of the head from a middle-aged Filipina co-worker. When the young man wasn't checking out our little train wreck he would read or possibly just pretend to read a magazine he must have carried with him. He looked simultaneously knowing and curious. Or was I reading too much into his eyes? Even if, as Evelyn complained, I dismiss people too quickly, I also have a habit of smelling the daffodils while a skunk crosses the road. For all I knew the magazine was a *Hustler* and he carried a pocket full of eviction notices he'd resume serving on the working poor after finishing his bagel. In any case, my immediate goal was to get away from my self-absorbed stud who droned on, smirking and sneering, stuck in a curious fusion of turbulence and monotony. I recalled a scene with Woody Allen sitting forlornly on a train, his fellow passengers a collection of grotesque losers. Inside another car parked on the next track, elegant, glamorous people frolic. A gorgeous blonde gestures to Woody as his own train pulls away. My train.

Rick didn't seem to notice that I no longer interrupted his soliloquy with questions or comments. I checked in on it from time to time but mostly let my mind drift. While rushing to this flop of a rendezvous, I'd miraculously missed slamming into a Prius full of Unitarians pulling out of a church parking lot. The averted catastrophe was a piece of good luck, and recalling it, I chuckled. Not a full-out laugh or anything, just a brief snicker of vocalized good cheer that escaped without warning. Okay, it was a borderline giggle and probably puzzling, but laughter's a primarily positive act, isn't it? Then I heard Rick ask me, "You're not, you know, laughing at me, are you?" Crap. What a nightmare. I shouldn't have reminded him of my presence. It seemed to work out better when he confined the conversation to himself. "You mind my asking you something?" he continued in a new, flatter tone. A deepening nightmare.

"I wasn't laughing at you. Really."

He seemed to accept that. But he started asking about my tattoo. Pick anything else—my job, attitude, hair style, plans for the future, anything. Don't focus on a mistake.

Just then a statuesque Asian housewife and her two toddlers sat down at the little table crowded next to ours, her arrival accompanied by thumping and unsnapping of belongings as she tended to her duties with workmanlike precision. Rick's gaze shifted just like that to her breasts. Like mine, they were no more than a B cup. And all this time I'd assumed boob fanatics were attracted to nothing less than a C. Maybe it was my imagination, but he also glanced at the little girl as though she were a steak he'd like to defrost some years down the road. I checked the time on my cell phone again. Nine more minutes.

◈

True, pretending to find an urgent text message wasn't a terribly original idea, and yes, I turned out to be a remarkably lousy actress. But I assumed he'd accept the polite fib so we could both continue our lives separately with only mild injuries. Nothing doing. He switched modes instantly, and before I understood what was happening he was ridiculing me with shocking dexterity, but not for long, because then he went off like an I.E.D: "Okay, Miss Hotshit. But *you* don't, you know, walk out on *me. I*—" He jumped to his feet, upsetting the table and knocking over cups, saucers, etc. The clumsiness of the move must have made him even more anxious to get out of Dodge, which he did, leaving me with coffee splattered across my white jersey and just about everyone in the Farmers Market food court staring.

The neighboring mother shook her head in disgust and wordlessly snapped to work, mopping both me and the table with napkins.

LENNY

Next thing I knew I was lifting her newly baptized leather purse from the wet floor and placing it on the table. The young mother had already squared everything else away.

"I've had much worse dates than that," I said.

No reply. It was as though she'd just been hit by a car and looked up from the pavement to find herself on stage before a sold-out audience. I noticed her left eyebrow was slightly, almost imperceptibly higher than the right. It was chiefly responsible for the somewhat sardonic look I'd seen just before rage-man lost control.

The neighboring mother, no doubt feeling mighty waves of sisterhood in the aftermath of all the recent male brutishness, glared at me like I was Charles Manson's nastier little brother.

RUTH

For months now I'd trudged through a dismal succession of yuppie men whose voices rose at the end of each sentence, turning everything they said into a questionable supposition. ("So I asked Human Resources to show me this so-called clause?") These streams of interrogatory inflections signaled that the speakers weren't committed to anything they said and that anyone who challenged their remarks was probably, they'd be the first to admit, on firmer ground. Then came Rick, who raised disappointment to a towering new level. "You know," he'd explained with remarkable coolness just before the explosion, "I tried to be nice to you. I even pretended you weren't a pathetic, deluded cunt. If I'd treated you like the loser you are, you'd be sucking my cock." Later I wondered whether this vile bastard had *discerned* something. Maybe I *was* a pathetic deluded cunt. It's so hurtful to know there are damaged people running around with such formidable talent for inflicting pain. Rick had opened the door just a crack to the deeper calamities that wait for the deserving and undeserving alike. Something awful could happen any time. Earthquake, leukemia, machete attack, boiler explosion. It's all out there, striking random souls right now, and maybe you're next.

◆

I got away from there just shy of ramming speed, letting the scarred stranger accompany me back to my truck. My no-nonsense new friend the Asian mother clearly disapproved, and I knew I was dizzy and vulnerable, but he felt safe to me.

L.A.'s ceaseless sunshine can make everything appear harmless despite the Ricks. Somehow the ludicrousness of the encounter pierced all the mannered foolishness that prevents most of us from talking turkey most of the time, and as we threaded our way through shoppers and vendors I found myself speaking naked truth to a stranger I knew nothing about.

"Some people just don't own that gene on the chromosome that's supposed to tell them this person's not interested in that particular topic so they should find another one or at least shut up. I'd worked past his studs and boots and twitches and all that. But he just kept checking out—oh, Christ, I don't even want to talk about it. And so what am I doing? Talking about it. I apologize. I'm babbling. I'm—oh my God, I'm doing it. You don't want to hear this, and I'm just being another Rick. I'm so sorry. I'm—"

"No, no you're not. I swear. I'm interested. Please, babble on."

"Good. Where was I?"

"He kept checking out something."

"Right, the tattoo, and . . . the area around it. But when you won't even let the other person leave, that's off the charts. How much—" And *that*'s when I started sobbing. Not when I was actually living the Rick experience, but only after I'd tried to explain its wretchedness to this nameless bagel consumer walking me to my car. A very young bagel consumer, too. But at least that made him less likely to be a married sneak. That's one way to avoid them. Find yourself a sophomore. I sensed he wanted to comfort me but knew better than to touch me.

Fortunately my crying was only a quick sun shower.

"Wait, wait, wait a minute," he said, stopping next to the fruit and vegetable stalls at the edge of the parking area. He had a trace of a foreign accent—too faint for me to identify. Another little mystery along with the scars. "May I speak frankly?" he asked me.

"I thought we *were* speaking frankly."

LENNY

"What tattoo?" I asked her. A white lie. I had in fact spotted it, but paid it only scant attention as I was too busy checking out her weightless walk, open smile, sweet hint of décolletage, and the discreet, alluring scent of her that was more discernible now that I'd convinced her to stop cantering. At some point it struck me that she could be a loon who enjoyed making scenes, maybe even a fiend who'd diabolically created all that furor back there in order to kick-start a conversation with me, turning this Rick person, conceivably a perfectly innocent soul, into a kind of human sacrifice. A subject I knew something about. But those were real tears. To fake all this she'd have to be a terrific actress. Of course we *were* in Hollywood.

"You didn't see it? It's—" She briefly glanced at her tattoo and didn't finish the sentence.

"Here's the problem," I said. "It's only natural now for me to check out—well—the tattoo. But not if it threatens to place me in the same category as—"

"Rick."

"As it stands now, I'm forced to look everywhere but in the direction of what we're talking about. It's really uncomfortable."

"It's your own fault for not taking a quick glance when you had the chance. I'll describe it, okay? A dumb little cartoon tortoise."

"May I take a fast sweep? It hurts my neck to keep it so rigidly focused on your forehead."

She moved out, resuming the same beastly pace. "Did you catch it this time?"

"Mmm hmm."

"I'm not blushing, am I?"

"A little. But the tortoise—"

"Maybe we could switch topics?"

"Excellent. It's just that—"

"You have no other topics?"

"Plenty, I've got plenty of topics."

"Excellent. By the way, it was kind of you not to point out how desperate I must have been to set up a date over the Internet. I guess most people meet people where they work, but that doesn't work for me." She nodded her head a couple of times. "I know, like—this Internet stuff works better?" She laughed. I liked hearing her laugh. "And please don't ask me where I work or where I'm from or—I don't want to start all that who, what, when, where crap, okay? I can't do it twice in one day. You don't know how bad this dating thing gets after years and years of it."

"Yes I do."

She stopped again, looking directly into my face, squinting one eye clownishly. I spied a hint of down above her upper lip. Face it, I decided. She's adorable.

"You're a mere pup," she said finally.

"I'm older than I look."

"I'm twenty-seven," she said, cantering again.

"Older. I mean I'm older, not—"

"Okay, so I'm twenty-nine," she said.

"I'm older. I swear it."

"How old then? I mean, what's the big secret? I told you my age, sort of."

"Well, I—"

"I'm thirty-one," she said. We were no longer under a canopy but moving across asphalt baked with sun. "Admit it, okay? You're twenty-four. It's nothing to be ashamed of. It's a nice age."

"You'd be surprised how old I am. Honest. But tell me, think we'll live happily ever after?"

"Possibly, but not together."

"You never know," I said.

"The things about which we most often jest are generally, on the contrary, the things that embarrass us."

"You can't frighten me off with your esoteric quotations."

"What's it take, then?"

"I'll tell you when I know you better."

"Don't be smug."

"I can take the personal criticism," I told her. "But shouldn't you know my name first?"

"Not necessarily. You could be a cad, you know."

"Smile when you say that."

"I am smiling."

"I know. I'm just babbling. Look, I loved your honesty back there. And I don't know this Rick, never spoke with him, but I can tell you that under ordinary circumstances . . . who knows? Maybe he's not so terrible."

"Ordinary circumstances?"

"What I mean is, a very pretty woman will do that to a guy. Make him trip all over himself. Like I'm doing right now while you force me to gallop."

"What? I'm supposed to feel guilty that he splashed coffee all over me? And it's not a gallop. It's only a fast clip."

"Look, we've been through a . . . *thing* together, and we can move completely past this Rick person. Fine with me. But see, that could have the opposite effect. It could—"

"Magnify his importance?"

"Exactly. But what I really wanted to say is, we should see each other again, don't you think? And I'll try to ignore how pretty you are so maybe I can stop stumbling around and talk the way I normally talk and we could see how that works. Or something."

"I know how the species works and all that, but if you came over to help because you liked the way I looked, well, don't plain-looking people deserve a little humanity too? *More* humanity?"

"I think . . . I hope I'd have helped if you looked like Eleanor Roosevelt. But I don't want to lie and say for sure when I don't know for sure."

We reached her vehicle, a little Ford Ranger pickup.

"Look," I said, "the circumstances were a little odd, but I'm glad we met, and I want to see you again. We can meet in a public place. This one's fine. For coffee, okay? And if you like, I'll bring character witnesses."

She studied my face some more, maybe still trying to guess my age. "Sure, we can have coffee. But I'm already wearing coffee, and I'm late for something."

She was lying, of course, but I didn't blame her. She fished out her keys.

"How can I find you?"

"Give me your number," she said.

Uh oh, trouble I hadn't seen coming, this tactic employed by hard-driving twenty-first-century women who ran marathons and global corporations and, theoretically at least, called men instead of the other way around. But it could be a ruse to ditch me without any messy confrontations like the one she'd just endured with Rick. And even if she were sincere, this liberated woman might feel decidedly less liberated when it came time to make the call. *Remember me?* So potentially embarrassing. Borderline desperate. The phone mission could easily slide south on her things-to-do list, ranking right around scrubbing the toilet. After a week or ten days of procrastinating, this woman whose name I didn't know would be afraid I'd forgotten her or changed my mind or moved in with my girlfriend. But if I insisted on getting her number she might chuck me into the slush pile with potential rapists and desperate bores.

She opened the door. The passenger compartment was oven temperature. She rolled down both windows before sliding in. I tore a page off my magazine, wrote down my name and number and handed it to her before firing one last shot. "Proust," I said.

"That's your name?" She was seated now, key in the ignition.

"'The things about which we most often jest.' It's from Proust."

"It just came to you?"

"No, I saved it to finish strong."

Starting her engine, she stuck out her lower lip and nodded, a gesture that seemed to indicate she was impressed, but I couldn't tell for sure. "I'm Ruth," she said, backing out.

She had my name on the scrap of paper, but I yelled it out anyway, which seemed appropriate until I heard myself.

❖

"She was being ironic," I told Jubal. I found him that night at his usual spot in Pamela's, his girlfriend's bar. "She thinks I'm a jerk. That's what it meant, didn't it? When she made the face."

"You're the one that saw it. *You* have to judge."

"She was laughing at me. She won't call."

"Yes she will. But from what you're saying, that could bring you a whole new set a troubles. You *do* know what I'm talking about."

I took a sip of the wretched house cabernet his girlfriend doled out to unsuspecting customers and dolts like me who knew what to expect but ordered it anyway.

"'Cause if she made that scene in Farmers Market just to meet you, man, she's trouble."

"A scheming, heartless bitch," I said. "Unless—" I paused.

"Unless what?"

"Unless maybe if that's what she did—and I'm not saying it is—I could also admire her courage."

"Man, I served in the Marine Corps with plenty of guys who had courage and also happened to be some of the biggest assholes on the planet. Courage is good only if it's *used* for something good. Hitler won an Iron Cross in World War I, the little cocksucker."

"I just hope she calls." Because of the bizarre circumstances surrounding our encounter, there was no casual stage. We'd gone straight to premature intensity. I should have addressed the problem more adequately when she was still in my sights. As usual, instead of acting intelligently when it counted I was poking through the ashes of my blunders. But I also knew there was no chance I could be honest with her anyway. Her doubts were well-founded, and I already regretted those happily-ever-after hints because I had no such intentions. I was a serial escape artist. Two, three dates at the most, and I'd be a trail of dust.

Chapter 2

Lenny

Ask yourself what you'd do if somewhere in the vastness of the data-sphere one of the electronic gizmos hiccupped and inexplicably moved a magnificent sum into your bank account. Would you demand an investigation? Or quietly hunker down with your loot and wait to see what happens? Ultimately I hunkered down. No one came for me. The Lord saved me, and, like a distracted banking computer, forgot about me. As far as I could tell. You could call me an eternal flame or a living monument to His mercy, but I expected I was merely the recipient of a sum serendipitously moved into the wrong column, a crumb dropped unnoticed in a kitchen crevice.

My memories—so many generations' worth—bounce about in a teasing, unsorted mess, sometimes leaping straight at me, sometimes streaking into the distance. I never know when I'll glance at something that lights a fuse to a long-dormant recollection, like the time I saw a cello and remembered I knew how to play it and how and when I learned, except the memories had spaces between them, parts I couldn't distinguish from dreams or the stories of others.

I've accumulated more regrets during my forty-odd centuries than a decent man could live with, partly because there were so many times I had to act without the luxury of certainty. I can still recall the Hohenzollern prince, for example, who might or might not have discovered my embezzlement. There was no time to sort out the clues before my dagger pierced his throat. I was saddened by the disillusion in his eyes, but I knew there was no mercy behind them either. He'd had men—and women too—tortured and murdered for offenses far less serious. There was no chance I could bargain away my transgression because everything I took I'd already given away, having long since lost interest in accumulating personal wealth. It's only by distributing largesse that I've prevented remorse for my thousand-times-a-thousand errors from smothering me. Understand that I have no special powers, don't leap buildings with a single bound. Cut me and I bleed.

You could argue that the extra portion of years I'd already enjoyed made the prince's life more precious than mine, particularly given my history as a fool driven by anger, avarice, conceit, cowardice, and a host of other frailties. It took me a long string of conventional lifetimes to acquire a degree of wisdom that others attain in only a standard go-around.

But I knew at the outset I must keep my secret, even from kindred souls. It was difficult, particularly at first. Divulging a confidence is part of what makes us human. But if I told others or stayed in one place too long I'd be taken for a witch or a demon, an obvious patsy to be blamed for whatever troubled those around me. If they didn't murder me at once they'd murder me later, quite possibly after worshiping me first. I'm not sure which would be more objectionable. I recall a tale I heard about tribesmen in South America who, conceivably well-intentioned, sawed a stranger in half and sewed him back together. They wanted to see whether he'd revive.

Centuries of observation have impressed me with the infinite range of murderous human pathology. No one raised moral questions when men built giant catapults to toss huge, flaming projectiles at the walls of cities to help them smash their way inside to rape, torture, plunder, enslave, and massacre the inhabitants. Historians who look back from what's advertised as a more sophisticated perspective don't even find these sieges curious. After all, that's what men do. But long ago a woman I loved pointed out that within those doomed cities were virtuous souls who sacrificed themselves to help others they cared about. To this day the wisdom of her words gives me a measure of hope even as leaders of what passes for civilization make artful excuses to perpetrate newer versions of the same old outrages.

As I moved from place to place I learned I must always blend in to some degree. Keeping to oneself invites scrutiny. I won't even guess how many languages I've learned or half-learned and forgotten as I wandered the Earth. I once stayed somewhere along the sea, in France, I think, where the landlord had stretched a wire just above the balcony rail to keep seagulls from setting down. Sometimes it seems all the resting spots are wired off and there's no place to set down and breathe. So a man just keeps moving.

I can't afford to gamble for my freedom with someone like the prince because protracted imprisonment would peel away my secret in layers, turning me into cornered, naked prey. That's always been my Achilles' heel. (No, my path never crossed Achilles'. He's merely a legend to me, just as I'm a legend to others. I expect the myth surrounding his life and death is at least as confused and inaccurate as mine.)

◈

When I first realized my unique status I prayed to heaven, hollered, meditated, wailed, studied, beseeched. *Remember me? Isaac. I'm still here. Why? What's it mean?* Think about being obsessed with something—truly obsessed—ten, fifty, a hundred years, then more hundreds. Eventually I placed the puzzle of my existence on a shelf. I remained aware of it, and it still haunted me, but it no longer tormented me. After all, I'd won a precious gift. If winning makes you sad, when do you get happy? It was a Samaritan girl who taught me this. I remember her sweet laughter as we made love and her red, wooly hair. I remember them as though it were no more than a couple of centuries ago. That's a joke. There's no joking in the bible. It wasn't exactly written by Jack Benny. Still, people in biblical times did crack jokes. Sometimes a sense of humor was downright indispensable, then as now. For example, there was that time the Lord ordered Saul to attack the Amalekites, to "utterly destroy all that they have, and do not spare them. But kill both man and woman, infant and nursing child." But Saul, cutting corners, spared the best of the tribe's sheep and oxen—and also their King Agag—because in those days too there were well-meaning souls who assumed it's okay to improvise sometimes, that you don't have to take God literally all the time. Nothing doing. Samuel, the Lord's prophet and presumed spokesman, informed Saul that his rebellious acts made him unfit to be king over all of Israel. To illustrate his point, Samuel "hewed Agag in pieces before the Lord in Gilgal." Now *that's* how you interpret an order. See what I mean? If you didn't laugh, you'd have to cry. Saul may very well have cried when he learned his kingdom would be smaller than he'd counted on. He was terribly ambitious.

◈

The Samaritan girl pitied me for the forlorn soul I was and also discerned that I held some singular status in the cosmos. The aging process is more than just a chemical formula. Life paints a portrait across the canvas of the soul. Thinning, silvered hair, the discolorations and creases verify a person's history. My face and body, though natural in appearance, failed to match my experiences, creating a dissonance that particularly sensitive individuals sometimes perceived. The Samaritan girl was among them. When I reached over to make love to her again she said, "You're older than you look, aren't you?"

"Isn't this an odd time to say so? I'm trying—"

"I know what you're trying. Quit it and answer the question."

"Yes."

"Yes what?"

"Yes, I'm older than I look."

"Do you believe that life is suffering?"

"Of course."

"Really?"

"You're making me suffer right now."

"Forget that and answer the question. Is life suffering?"

"No."

"I don't think so either. But my mother does." She caressed my brow and looked at me with great seriousness and tenderness as she said, "She says the gods make us suffer, and that I'm witless not to see it. You do suffer though, don't you?"

"Some."

"You don't have to," the Samaritan girl said. "No one, not even the gods, can make us suffer unless we let them." She saw my confusion. "We can't stop them from doing their worst, but only our minds can allow us to suffer. If you understood that, really understood it, you could endure eternity if you had to. You'd see it's not a curse, as my mother would think. It's a blessing. Can you believe that?"

"I think so."

"Think about it some more. Do you promise?"

"I promise."

"Good, but do it later." She thrust her loins against mine and said no more about eternity or suffering. I left her one of the best dogs I ever owned. Still, her kinsmen chased me for weeks. As I recalled her assurances, her smile, and her laughter I remembered what she told me, and eventually I came to terms with the special nature of my existence.

Maybe I was that tree that falls alone in the forest with no one to hear. Perhaps a joke of some kind or the subject of a bet between God and Satan—as was Job when they turned his family, servants, and possessions into casino chips while using him as a now-celebrated lab rat. In fact, you could say neither God nor Satan gave a rat's ass about any of them.

Satan we understand. More troublesome is the God who, as Dostoevsky pointed out with such thundering dismay, allows infants to be abused and slaughtered even before they get a chance to sin. Amalekite infants, for example.

But if I had the opportunity to get answers from somebody, I'm not even sure God would be my first choice. Because let's not forget my father, who, I'm not the first to note, was so matter-of-factly willing to butcher me on behalf of his unseen master. When Abraham took me up to Mount Moriah, Moses had yet to receive the law on Mount Sinai. Abraham, revered down through time for doing what he was told, was God's obedient servant even before the terms of obedience were spelled out. Ironically, it was my father who taught me compassion for the unfortunate. But mostly he was a close-mouthed man who, except for his detailed instructions on tending our flocks, provided remarkably little guidance, especially for a prophet.

I myself never had the feeling someone was watching out for me or watching at all, really, unless you count The Beast. More on him later. Rambling through time, minute by minute, century after century, I saw no evidence I had any divine role or purpose and always knew I was mortal, that something or someone would eventually kill me. Though it's unlikely any other human has eluded death as long as I have, and though everyone else seems, relatively speaking, to drop dead shortly after birth, sometimes it appeared that I was the only soul aware that the trap is set not just for thee but also the generic *me*—that is, everybody. The post-traumatic stress disorder experienced after battle is egregious to its sufferers because their survival triggers not delight but guilt and shame. It also yanks them out of their insane trust that tomorrow will be there for them. I have no such trust, but the Samaritan girl showed me a path, a way to expunge guilt and shame and to endure.

Some of the same people who assume the bible is an archaic collection of fairy tales beneath serious consideration have no qualms obeying a self-proclaimed priestess from the lost continent of Atlantis. Trying to sort out the validity of different mythologies is like asking why a raven is like a writing desk. They all require some faith in the paranormal, don't they?

I *know* the paranormal exists because I'm the proof. Aside from The Beast I may be the only being on Earth who could say with any certainty that there is a God, or at the very least there was at one time someone or something with the power to cast this curious spell over my life—a mysterious being who spoke to my father but left me as uninstructed as the fools and charlatans who claim special knowledge of His divine strategy. Even so, you might expect that after all this time I'd have more of these metaphysical questions figured out. But look around and you see that relative longevity provides only limited advantage in solving them.

Experience has taught me that even when I have little appetite for the future the indifference or despondency will pass. And after finding Ruth I looked forward to seeing her again, needed to, in fact, remembering everything she said and the fetching way she said it, visualizing her face as I stared at my cell phone to make it ring. Even if she did steamroll over hapless Rick to get to me, he was still a fool to give up so easily.

You may be asking yourself why I squandered my time on such trivial matters. After all, I'm Isaac, one of history's most enduring figures. Couldn't I find more important things to think about? I should have cured the common cold by now. Certainly a more fitting recipient could have been found for my gift, but given the fact that billions of souls sleep on the hungry edge of death night after night, any fair-minded person who compares what people get with what they deserve can only conclude that fate is a sociopath. Furthermore, Ruth, I suspected, was nowhere near trivial.

CHAPTER 3

RUTH

"How soon can I see you?" A sweet remark he sweetly made. I'd waited only two days to call, sending a signal by subtracting a day from the most widely accepted interval.

"This whole month looks bad," I told him. "How's two weeks from Thursday?"

Silence. Then: "Wait a minute. You're kidding, right?"

"I'm kidding. There's a Starbucks at Melrose and Robertson. Can you be there in an hour?"

After only an hour or so together it felt like home. There was just enough positive tension between us to keep our senses pleasingly taut. As an unusually gentle Ray Charles CD played in the background, I kvetched a little about life as a freeway flyer in the Cal State University system but didn't get into anything deep. I bought the CD before we left.

LENNY

I'd feared some of the hard truths she shared the day of her disaster date would embarrass her and make her circumspect. But she was open and unafraid. We both recognized the bridge connecting us was made of firmer stuff than the ugly scene that brought us together. Of course beneath my own openness, as always, hid the great lie. Later, when I would close my eyes to relive perfect moments with Ruth, letting them float from past to future and back to the present like serene shadows, watching her glide toward me in that coffee shop was one of those perfect moments.

RUTH

Once we were inside my apartment the element of privacy made us more conscious that our flesh had yet to touch. The mutual telepathy was so strong I felt we might start to levitate. At some point we read the CD booklet together on the sofa, our faces level. He reached out and gently touched my hair. I touched his. Shortly thereafter we fell into bed, which is not my standard operating procedure. Lenny was funny and beautiful and had me convinced I was too. We rushed the tail end of our mating dance (pun intended) when I heard Evelyn's key in the lock, a comical but exasperating juncture because we finished with a wondrous bilateral orgasm but had no time to savor it. Home early from associate-producing TV's last-surviving soap opera, Evelyn was aware that I barely knew Lenny, which is what panicked me. He looked at me like I was nuts as I signaled quiet, fishing clothes off my bedroom floor at two hundred miles an hour. Poor Lenny, he didn't know the walk to the living room would carry him straight into an airplane propeller.

We should have either left immediately or just stayed in my room, but somehow ended up sitting across from Evelyn in the living room. He smiled through several minutes of her passive aggression before striking back. Ostensibly they were disagreeing over the relative morality of feeding Hollywood vulgarity to the masses, and I doubt I heard any fresh ideas from either of them in the eternal debate over art versus prostitution. But the real dispute was over the audacity of what we all knew had just occurred in my room.

"Look," she said, "you asked me so I told you. Yes, we get screwball letters. Yes, we pass them around. It's what happens on soaps."

"Okay, but these delusional people who write letters of advice to the show's characters are *not* darling. They're not even distant cousins to anything darling. They're dangerous imbeciles."

"Dangerous? Don't be silly."

"They register to vote," he said.

"True, and they are imbeciles, but at least they know how to button their shirts." Crap! Lenny looked down helplessly at his errant buttons hopelessly buttoned inside the wrong holes and grinned a mischievous grin. I giggled, but it came out like an alien screech. Evelyn pressed her advantage: "So I'm an enemy of civilization for working on a soap, but you're an agent of taste and discretion for cracking heads for whatever network piece of shit production needs hired bullies for the day."

"I don't crack heads or bully anybody." He said it like a hurt child. Lenny, we'd learned, worked for a firm that provided security for film and TV shoots around L.A. I reached over and squeezed his fingers. What the hell, a few minutes earlier we'd been mingling bodily fluids. But the gesture further isolated Evelyn, who said, "I suppose I could quit my job and go make tires in Columbus, Ohio like my mom. Except she worked in one of those Springsteen factories that aren't there anymore."

LENNY

Have you ever been wakened from a perfect dream by a demon jabbing you in the ass with a pitchfork? That's how it felt to slide out of bed with Ruth into the jaws of a man-eating roommate with a broken marriage. Why did I let her pull me into an argument? Because sometimes I'm stupid.

"Look, I'm sorry I insulted your livelihood," I told her. "But you—you were just so . . . it was my fault. Let's start again. My name's Lenny." I held out my hand in anticipation of a bony shake that didn't happen.

She lifted a nostril, wolf-like. "I was just so *what?*" Her chemically altered, reddish brown hair was a trifle dark for her complexion, and she was built like a fiber-optics wire, her skin stretched tight across her narrow face like silk on a loom. Walking around hungry wasn't helping her disposition. I'd find out later that Evelyn had been "a little heavy" when her husband split.

RUTH

Mumbling something about being hungry, we beat it out of there. Lenny took the freeway down to Hermosa Beach, where we ate on the patio of a little Vietnamese seafood place a few steps from the sand. Not far away sat two men and a woman, all in their thirties and carefully groomed in black business attire and shiny shoes. There along the beach they stood out like they were wearing Batman suits. They'd probably ducked out of a sales meeting. From what I picked up of the conversation, they didn't know each other terribly well. The woman was an attractive blonde who looked like she had a black belt in PowerPoint. The conversation was laced with terms like "customers" and "distribution," and the two men pretended that accompanying her to her room after dinner would never occur to them. It's not easy being a woman sometimes. But just then it felt awfully good to me. Trouble was, I had to set him straight on Evelyn.

"Hey, I already know you're not gay, remember?"

"Shut up," I said.

For a split second I was afraid he thought I was telling him to shut up in earnest, but I realized just as quickly that we'd fast-tracked nuances and were already past the possibility of such misunderstandings. Yet once you start telling the truth you lose control of the story. I found myself revealing secrets before we'd traded middle names.

"Ruth, please tell me you're making all this up."

"Of course I did. You think someone would really abandon a little girl at a carnival?"

"Yes," he said. His eyes and voice were so full of compassion and understanding. I took a bite of halibut just to give myself something to do and let loose a short burst of nervous laughter, nearly spraying bits of fish across the table. After getting all that under control, I told him, "It's okay, really. I don't remember any of it." I explained that the carnival was in a little town near the Mexican border. "It took the carnies a while to realize I was really alone because they said I wasn't crying, just walking around eating cotton candy. I must have been used to being alone. My picture went out everywhere, but no one knew who I was."

"Do you remember—"

"Nothing from that night or anything before it. The doctors figured I was just about two years old. I was clean and dressed neatly in a little blue Sears, Roebuck dress. No signs of abuse. I didn't know my last name."

"I—"

"Please don't make a big thing out of it. I know you're sorry, okay? But don't keep saying it. It wasn't your fault or my fault. I figure my parents or my mother or whoever it was just couldn't raise me, and they weren't terribly sophisticated about how to handle it. The sheriff's people thought I might have been from some polygamous Mormon sect. There were plenty around that part of Arizona. They're not fans of things like birth certificates."

"My father heard voices," he said suddenly.

"What about your mother?"

"She obeyed them."

"How did that turn out?"

"Not so bad. You want to come to my place?"

"How long does this date last anyway?"

"I'll take you home if you want."

"Evelyn gets protective because she thinks I must be fragile from all those foster homes. She's like family, but I can never figure out if she's a sister or a mother. It's not what I was looking for when I advertised her room on Craigslist. I know she's a little screwed up, but I love her."

"How *were* those foster homes?"

"Not so bad. Let's go to your place."

He lived in Manhattan Beach in an area full of enormous homes that use every inch of space because they're on pint-sized lots that were originally laid out for little beach cottages. Now there are all these monster houses shoulder-to-shoulder. Pointless castles encasing pointless space. They say family members find each other by calling room to room on their cell phones.

Lenny's guest quarters consisted of a couple of rooms inside a sort of Greco-Roman, over the top, *Gone with the Wind* manor owned by a Hollywood producer who lived there with his personal assistant and consecutive concubines. Lenny's section was, like his pristine Chevrolet, too deper-sonalized to say much about his inner life. I got the feeling he didn't have much stuff inside the drawers or closets. The owner was a client of his employer, and Lenny had some sort of deal that allowed him to live there rent-free. What else did I know about Lenny? He had a collection of mysterious but not disfiguring scars, he wore a thin, metal band above one elbow that I decided to classify as intriguing rather than puerile, he had a trace of an accent I still couldn't identify, his father used to hear voices, and I was already nuts about him. He was simultaneous excitement and warmth. Sure of himself but not conceited. I wanted to know everything about him, but I didn't want to nag or break the spell with a conversational application form.

"Are you browsing my books or examining them for evidence?" he asked me.

I decided to answer by continuing to read the page in front of me. The collection was mostly contemporary novels.

"Sorry I don't have more. I send out for just enough to put one over on literate ladies. What color are your eyes?" He came over and brushed the back of my neck with his fingers. I instantly got weak in the knees. "Hey, what are you laughing about?"

"I'm just happy to be here." I said.

"Me too."

I threw the book on the sofa. "Can I take a shower?" I asked him.

He began gently unbuttoning my blouse.

"I'll take that as a yes. My eyes are gray. That's why they seem to change color."

"Your nipples have a hint of orange to them. Citrus."

We went straight from the shower to bed, but we didn't have sex. Not exactly, anyway.

"I'm not normally this easy," he said.

"But you seem curiously proficient at removing other people's shirts and tossing them on the floor."

"I resent that. You know, your eyes do change color."

"Told you. A lot of people around the Baltic have gray eyes. I could be Estonian or something. But maybe not. Athena had gray eyes."

"Athena?"

"The goddess of heroic endeavor. She lived a long way from the Baltic. Can I see that bracelet thingy on your arm?"

He held it out for me, nuzzling me with his lips.

"It looks pretty old."

"I know it looks peculiar," he told my neck. "It's my good luck charm." Looking up, he added, "You look so sweet with your hair wet, like a flower after the rain."

"Why does this Hollywood big shot let you live here for free?"

"So he won't be quite so nervous. These producers start to believe their own dreck TV shows, where nobody dies in bed. They all expect to be killed by terrorists or abducted by a gang of criminals. . . . Something."

"Led by a diabolical mastermind."

"Of course. They have only two plots."

"Isn't it a little intrusive, living with your boss? Or I guess he's just sort of a boss."

"I don't run his errands or wash his socks. I go weeks without seeing him. He doesn't even have the key to my entrance."

"Stop that, please." He was tonguing my navel.

"You don't like it?"

"It tickles, and I'm trying to gather intelligence."

"I can see that. For who? Evelyn?"

"Maybe. You have an accent. I can't place it. Don't do that, either. Crap, please don't do that."

"Is this our first argument?"

I jumped his mouth with my lips and teeth and after a while pulled back. "What was the question?" I asked him.

"Whose question?" Our mouths barely touched. His lips were a sweet breeze across mine.

"I forget."

Okay, so we did have sex again. Neither of us was hungry for it this time. It was more like a mutual confession that we couldn't get enough of each other. Eventually we lay under a sheet half-watching his little TV.

"I'm from Israel," he said. "Originally. But I also lived in Europe."

"Is that how you got your job? Because you were some kind of commando?"

"Commandos work in close. I was artillery. If the enemy's within five or ten kilometers, we made a mistake. I work in a library too."

"Doing security?" I found his palm and held his hand as I turned on my side to face him.

He shook his head and smiled. "Normal library work." I wondered what training he might have had to be a librarian, but decided to interrogate him no further.

When he drove me home neither of us felt compelled to make conversation. My apartment was in one of those standard Southern California buildings with open walkways looking down on a pool. He walked me to the door, and when I fished the key out of my purse he took my face in his hands, kissing me gently. I wrapped my arms around his neck. Everything was good. Everything.

CHAPTER 4

LENNY

My boss Zev was part of a loose regiment of the Israeli diaspora whose members want the world to believe they are or were at one time connected to the Mossad. Zev carefully cultivated a tabloid image of quiet cunning and capability by never answering questions about his personal history. Phone conversations at his end consisted of "Okay," "No," and terse grunts. He pumped iron five days a week and it showed. Rarely would his face show any expression. Some days I'd be certain he was a phony. Other days I wasn't so sure. But even if he wasn't the real thing, Zev knew how to find it, having assembled an overqualified crew of folks who knew their business. Just about all our work was related to the entertainment industry. Mostly we protected camera crews on streets that depicted foreboding, delight, squalor, luxury, or whatever else the script demanded. We also ferried celebrities' kids around town, taking Hollywood princelings from school to Little League or diet counseling or wherever they were going, while their parents got massaged or analyzed or shot up with human growth hormones that were fast becoming essential pharmacological agents around the "industry," as it's called in L.A. Based on their prodigious efforts in pursuit of eternal youth, they deserved it far more than I did.

❖

When Tamara's brother Miguel saved me I was on the street, ragged and hungry, hoping to get to Portugal, where it was rumored the king protected Jews. I had to stay clear of roving packs of thugs checking for circumcisions. All along the way they were torturing and burning secret Jewish *Marranos* and no doubt many genuine *conversos* as well, particularly those with property. I vividly recall the stink of charred flesh. Some victims were baked in brick ovens. The cruelty was overwhelming. Beyond understanding. All around me was desperation, resignation, anger, and madness. I'd lost people you could call my friends, though I generally tried not to make friends.

Miguel happened upon me shortly after I'd escaped capture by a notoriously vicious bishop in Toledo. One of his thugs managed to slash my thigh before I killed him. It still bled sporadically. I'd used the last of my coins for wine, but it was all gone now and I was seated in the dirt, my head in my hands. Miguel stopped his oxcart and invited me to his home. I gambled he was a Jew helping his own kind rather than an Inquisition bounty hunter. I soon discovered he was an actual Christian, the kind that aids strangers.

Tamara's mother asked no questions as she sewed up my wound. She and the rest of the family treated me with instinctive trust and respect. Next morning after breakfast I limped outside to work in their olive grove, but they commanded me to rest. To this day I never got to Portugal.

Tamara had a broad face, perhaps homely in a certain light, but she had a lovely, open smile. She would grow comelier as years passed, though I could never convince her of that. At first she treated me like one of her brothers, teasing me about my scruffy condition and shoving me about with a saucy smile. You already have brothers, I whispered to her, and they love you, as well they should, but I adore you. "Behave yourself," she said, but we both knew she was mine. Her parents accepted it too even though I refused baptism.

Every evening, following our simple meal, Tamara would tell us tales. At first I was startled to hear a young girl take on this august role, but with her angelic voice and calm, unfaltering demeanor, she had her little audience always eager for the next word. Her stories were about a handsome adventurer named Tobias who traveled to strange lands on a headstrong little mare named Carlita. One day, wandering into a secluded valley, Tobias had shared a cabbage with Carlita that he purchased from a mysterious one-legged woman in a crowded market. After taking one bite Carlita owned gifts of both speech and prophesy, pronouncing future events to Tobias in a sweet singing voice. Sometimes her prophesies came in the form of riddles whose meaning wouldn't become clear until later. Thanks to Carlita's gift and Tobias's courage they generally outmaneuvered a villainous duke named Rodrigo, who, after learning of Carlita's special powers, was obsessed with the idea of stealing her in order to vanquish rivals and amass a vaster fortune.

Carlita always needed a fresh cabbage whenever she and Tobias sought information about the immediate future. Cabbage was sometimes a scarce commodity. They'd also learned the hard way that for the magic to work, it must be Tobias who fed it to her. From time to time Tamara hinted at a melancholy longing between handsome, headstrong Tobias and feisty, clever Carlita. They finished each other's sentences. Tamara would continue the tale of Tobias and Carlita as long as I knew her, even on those rare nights we quarreled. We both knew that by the end of the chapter we'd be friends again.

Memory tricks us. People habitually look back fondly upon experiences that might have actually been unpleasant at the time. Not so my life with Tamara. The years were filled with joy and passion, but they also presented a gradual puzzle when they had no effect on my appearance. At first she blamed herself. Why did she look so old? She also blamed herself for being childless. I secretly looked upon that as a blessing. When the time came for me to leave her, she'd be in a worse fix with children to care for.

I knew better than to let a relationship linger, but I couldn't bring myself to give up Tamara. After we stayed with her family longer than I should have dared, I invented an excuse to take her a world away across the Pyrenees, where we established a new life in another cottage. I took a new name, and Tamara asked no questions, just as she'd asked me no questions years earlier when I'd shown up at her family's cottage with a sword wound. But now her stories of Tobias and Carlita weren't always as good-natured. Cruelty was more likely to get results, and Duke Rodrigo, aided by his cohorts, was less of a clown and more dangerous.

As time passed we refrained from speaking of the changes—and lack of them—that mocked us. In my heart I still saw Tamara as a beauty. A casual wink from her could lift my spirits for days. But she came to see herself as a kind of gremlin. She'd change her hair or try different clothes, and seeing no improvement, blame herself.

One cool summer night, Tamara, telling her story, said a plant disease was ravaging local crops, and that Tobias and Carlita had been unable to find a cabbage for weeks. They knew the duke's people were close. Finally they came upon an estate in terrible disrepair. The landlord, a curious, stinking bear of a man, may have been mad. He made vague threats he'd quickly apologize for, then start a new cycle of menace. Finally he agreed to trade his last cabbage for something Carlita dearly loved—her blanket. She'd had it since she was a filly. Desperate, they made the exchange.

When they found an isolated spot and Tobias fed her the cabbage, Carlita wept as she sang to Tobias that very soon Duke Rodrigo would slay him with a thrust of his sword, and hinted that this time they would be unable to change the future. Tamara, singing me this message in Carlita's voice, added that Tobias didn't protest, but accepted his fate. At that point, Tamara said, Carlita became ill and was soon racked with pain and nausea. Medicinal herbs had no effect. Tobias and Carlita feared she'd been poisoned, but neither dared say it aloud. Tamara halted her story, to be continued the next night.

I considered the thousands of times I wanted to speak of what we both saw—and all the times Tamara gazed in tortured wonder at my damned ageless self and all the times I pretended not to see. Crossing the mountains had been our tipping point. Since then we'd conversed only at superficial levels.

That night we lay awake listening to each other breathe, half-pretending to sleep. I was a wheelwright in those days, and the next afternoon, paying improper attention to my work, I broke my wrist. Tamara barely breathed as she bound it with a rag. After giving me herbs for the pain, she brushed my hair with her hand and smiled. I'd told her so many times how much I loved her, and I wanted to tell her then but something held me back. That night, continuing the story, she said Carlita's illness left her barely mobile. She and Tobias tried to hide in a cave, but Rodrigo's henchmen waited inside and surprised them, disarming Tobias. Rodrigo arrived, and with a grand flourish, he fed Carlita a cabbage he'd acquired for the occasion. "Sing!" he shouted. After anxiously repeating the command several times without success he broke into tears of rage and grief, believing that all his dreams were shattered. Despite their desperation, neither Tobias nor Carlita explained the cabbage must come from Tobias's hand. Finally the crazed duke thrust his sword straight at Tobias's throat. But with the last of her strength Carlita darted between them and took the blade deep in her chest. One of the duke's thugs, distraught to see the beautiful mare harmed, neglected to watch Tobias just long enough for him to grab the thug's sword and kill him with it.

The ground beneath Carlita was already soaked with her blood, and Tobias believed she was dead already. Or perhaps he wanted to believe it as a dozen soldiers ran at him. He grabbed the reins of a soldier's horse and rode off, barely making it out of the cave. The duke's surgeons couldn't save Carlita, who died with blood gurgling in her throat. Tobias rode straight back to the estate where he'd traded for the cabbage. Without hesitation he slew the landlord in front of his family, placed Carlita's blanket on his new mount, a sprightly mare, and rode off toward new adventures.

For several minutes Tamara and I said nothing. Then, her face blank, she returned to the story, telling me that later Tobias fed a cabbage to his new mare, whom he'd named Maria. Maria foretold the future in a lovely singing voice, just as Carlita used to do. Tamara described these events in a buoyant, enthusiastic tone that made them even more dreadful.

I tearfully begged Tamara to take back the story, to let Carlita live, and when she refused I lost control and slapped her. She slapped me back. "Coward," she said softly. "You're an evil wizard and a coward." I stepped out into the moonless night with my tears. Seated on a log, I stared into the blackness of a forest whose tallest trees had sprouted many centuries after my birth. I'm not sure how much time passed before Tamara joined me. She poured us wine, and both of us drank more than we were used to. I don't remember going back inside, but we both ended up on the straw mattress, and the candles were out. In utter darkness and without saying a word, we made love for the first time in years. The next morning she was gone, perhaps to return to her family, perhaps to die alone.

Chapter 5

Ruth

Evelyn: "I *know* you've asked him. Or at least hinted around. I mean it's such a basic question: 'How old are you?' Ruth, listen to me. This isn't right. It's—something's wrong."

I should have just lied to her, made something up. But I couldn't, and I was paying a price. "Something wrong would be lying to me. He's just not saying."

"And you don't think that's peculiar?"

"Of course I do, but it's not so awful. And I have to prepare for class tomorrow."

"Then get up early. This is important, okay? Because it sounds like he's some kind of loon."

"Skip is a loon. But you keep telling me to throw myself at him."

"Okay, he's a little eccentric. But he's no strangler."

"Neither is Lenny."

"Back up. I never told you to throw yourself at Skip. You don't have to. He's nuts about you."

"And he's solvent, right?" That made her smile. Much of the time she looked as though she'd just lost her keys down a manhole—or was ready to accuse someone of tossing them in. But Evelyn had a good heart. You just needed to steer her away from discussions about any man who reminded her even remotely of her ex-husband. Skip, my ex-boyfriend, didn't. He was, like me, another member of the stumbling surplus herd of Ph.D.'s and Ph.D. candidates who weren't science, software, or derivatives virtuosos, but hopelessly impractical humanities slugs. The hard facts of supply and demand forced us to settle for transitory jobs teaching basic courses to freshmen for part-time crumbs. In L.A. we'd even been given our own nomenclature—freeway flyers—as though we were a local basketball team. We scuttled from campus to campus earning a little here and a little less there and sharing our mandatory office hours in cave-like, windowless cubbyholes. No matter how many classes we taught we could never earn half as much as the tenured full-timers safe in their palace.

By training too many of us, they'd created tasks for themselves that kept their own jobs secure. Our expendable numbers wrecked our bargaining position, and we entered the working world as their bitches. One of my fellow flyers confided she felt like one of Charlotte Brontë's penniless governesses. Personally, I felt a kinship with Orwell, whose *Down and Out in Paris and London* related his bleary existence as a migratory pauper in Depression-era England, when towns steered unemployed tramps into an endless cycle of hunger and ejection. Their minds became fogged by the never-ending quest for the next charity morsel down the road, turning them into harmless, barking seals that must applaud their fish. We freeway outcasts frequently had more solid credentials than our putative betters behind the drawbridge, but once we became "adjunct" lecturers we could never win respectable positions from employers who'd seen us work the street.

Skip was a gentle man partial to baggy corduroys and scuffed shoes and unequipped to battle these institutional cruelties. Skip could never marry again. He told me that on our second date while I tried not to crack up. He was America's last obedient Catholic and took no notice of moneyed aristocrats who routinely obtained annulments after half a dozen kids so they could marry their receptionists or personal trainers.

About a year and a half before I met him, a teenage girl unwrapping a Hostess cupcake crashed her SUV into him on his bicycle, breaking seventeen of his bones and inflicting slight brain damage. Just before I broke up with him he'd won a $2.6 million settlement, minus a third to his lawyer. But I can almost guarantee he's still living on East Fountain above a Thai restaurant in a tiny little apartment that always smelled like peanut sauce. He paid rent ten days early every month so his landlord who never repaired anything wouldn't become upset with him. Skip needed the bike-crash bonanza to cushion him from the next disaster he knew must be somewhere over the horizon. He kept it all in insured certificates of deposit and a no-interest checking account, making him look like a financial genius when the world's economy melted down at the end of the George W. Bush administration. He was a kind though often preoccupied person who spent hours and hours doing puzzles—Rubik's Cubes, crosswords, you name it. He read magazines and books about puzzles and kept everything catalogued and stored precisely. His possessions were better organized than a Swiss bank and they were all vacuumed, scrubbed, and polished.

Skip must have been more of a regulation human being once. No one gives you a nickname like Skip if you're an eccentric loner. I think his name was a clue to why I'd stuck with him as long as I did. I'd hoped to bring back the more upbeat, daring Skip that had to be buried in there somewhere. He was extremely intelligent and had a dry wit he was too willing to turn on himself. Skip saw only parts of himself as they were, but then how many of us see ourselves as we truly are? At a crucial juncture of my work on Mary Shelley, he gave me remarkably insightful suggestions. He was a more astute scholar than most academic maestros with the authority to act on their opinions, and was a patient, wonderful teacher. But Skip was unlikely ever to fight his way off the freeway into a full-fledged faculty slot. Sadly, neither was I. Or at least so I thought at the time.

◆

I was feeling too good about Lenny to let Evelyn change my mind about him, but I didn't completely discount her comments. It was her friendship that made me realize I'd been starved my whole life for advice from someone who cared about me. Evelyn's school chums, she said, were coached by their mothers to barter their time-stamped tits and asses for matrimony with a well-connected frat boy. It's what she wanted too. "Fortunately," she said, "I had a wiser mom than that. She encouraged me to spread my wings. Our beliefs were transposed, me and my mom. The daughter's supposed to be the free spirit. The mom's the calculating bitch. We used to laugh about it."

Unfortunately, Evelyn's advice to me precisely mirrored the same foolish ideas she railed against now. "To thine own self be true," Polonius tells his son Laertes, but Polonius failed to notice that he himself was a duplicitous sneak who took none of his own counsel. Evelyn was Polonius's opposite. She lived honestly but gave rotten advice.

"How do you know he's not married?"

"I've seen his bathroom, remember?"

Evelyn closed her eyes and shook her head. "All right, he said he'd been in the IDF. They go in at eighteen or nineteen and come out in three years. When did he get out?"

"I don't know. What's the IDF?"

"Israel Defense Force. I dated an Israeli for almost a year before I met Ian. L.A.'s thick with them, you know."

"Really? Would you say Lenny's accent is Israeli?"

"Ah, you have doubts."

"Not true."

"Then why ask?" Getting no answer, she added, "I can't place it either. Look, Ruth, looked at from a certain angle, hiding his age is not such a big deal. I know that. I mean whatever the truth is, how bad can it be? The problem is—and I'm sure you already realize this—if he hides that, what else is he hiding?"

I wished I could faithfully transmit Lenny's sincerity—the honest center of him and all the sweet particulars that came with it. But even if I could, I needed to save at least some of that for myself, keep it nestled in a place that was mine alone. Let her win the debating points.

Okay, Lenny and I had only one date. But it was a twenty-four-hour date. That must be worth at least five or six standard dates. By that measure, sleeping with him wasn't even premature. I was even starting to love that imbecile Rick for bringing me into the Farmers Market on just the right day to run into Lenny.

And then, the next morning before I left for work, I got the call from Borges that, out of the blue, gave me reason to hope that my moribund academic prospects might rise in synch with my sweet romance.

LENNY

The last time I'd run into The Beast had been forty years earlier on the Chesapeake Bay. I was a mate on a waterman's paint-starved boat. That's what fishermen were called in those parts—watermen. We'd steam out of Annapolis into the cold morning darkness searching for fish, eels, crabs, oysters, whatever we could pull in with our traps, nets, hooks, and even a rifle when it made sense. But our ranks were thinning as monster factory vessels and chemical garbage plundered and poisoned the catch. The last watermen standing were scarred and rough, like Roman legionnaires. They'd mangle a finger or crack a rib and still move like cats along the rail. They couldn't swim. It was a tradition. You fall, you drown.

One day on shore we ran into a friend of the captain, a hunched, ape-like figure. I don't remember his face exactly, but he had a deep scar where one eyebrow used to be and a purplish thatch of nose hair. Within five minutes he was bragging about sucker-punching a tobacco farmer. "He says, 'All you watermen are full of it.' I hit him so hard, made him funny in the head. Heard his wife took him up to Baltimore for tests." You'd have thought he was describing the day he got the call from the Nobel committee. I envisioned the enormous, ape-like fist crashing into the life of the farmer-husband-father in an assault not intended as a lesson or retribution but merely as entertainment for the attacker. And suddenly I recognized him as The Beast. Speaking with his chin down like a boxer, leering up with his Rasputin eyes, waiting for me to recognize him. When I did it felt like being trapped inside a plunging elevator. He'd tricked me into speaking with him, something I'd never done in all the preceding centuries. I stumbled away too frightened to look over my shoulder. The Beast laughed and laughed, a hideous rattling sound fading in the distance.

I can't say why I recognize him because he takes on a new appearance each time he turns up. Back in the thirties he was a young soldier in the Red Army with dirt-caked hands and spidery veins on a hatchet face that showed no joy, grief, or compassion as he and another soldier seized a miraculously cheerful, sweet-faced boy peddling bread from a pushcart on a train platform. The boy was so desperate to escape that he tried to tear away his own scalp as the Beast, unappeasable, clutched him by the hair. An incongruent flower of a boy who'd somehow sprung from that gray, windswept place, he had a mongrel that yapped and jumped but like me did nothing as they tossed his master, now emitting pitiful, lamb-like sounds, into a freight car crowded with prisoners bound for Siberia. The two soldiers, I learned later, had taken a count and come up one convict short, so they grabbed the first fellow they saw. It could easily have been me. But The Beast chose another. Why? Why stalk me if he wasn't going to strike? He would, of course. He just wanted to make sure I was good and frightened first.

The guards had opened the door of the boxcar for only an instant, but the stench of excrement was unendurable. The inhabitants were startled like slumbering bugs, foul, filthy, barely human anymore as they mumbled curses at the terrified new passenger.

I've seen The Beast perhaps a dozen times over four thousand years, and no, I didn't know who he was. But he knew who I was. I was sure of it. Remember I mentioned a bishop inquisitor in Toledo? That was him too. Possibly The Beast had answers to the puzzle surrounding my existence, but when I spotted him I always got clear of him fast. I'd prepare myself to stand my ground next time, but when the moment came, uncompromising fear slammed into me with the power of a storm-fed surf. Racing away, I'd learn nothing once again.

There was plenty to ask him. First, who, precisely, was he? And what about me? Was there a purpose to the special nature of my existence? Was it something I must discover for myself? I'd never determined what I was supposed to do. I was a mystery to my own self. Of course there was always the possibility that he knew no more about me than I about him. If the ignorance were mutual, though, he ought to be curious about me, and he wasn't. Maybe he knew of other forgotten souls like me floating about the Earth. Maybe whatever made me the way I was had taken a radically different form or was long gone, leaving me a puppet without a puppet master, like one of those Japanese soldiers stranded on an island after World War II, comically, tragically waiting to hear from a power that no longer existed.

Did my father correctly identify the source of the voice that ordered him to slay me? And what about the presumed angel that stayed his hand? If the order to sacrifice me was a trick, the order to spare me might also have been a trick. Abraham could just as easily have been the butt of a joke as a prophet. I never got the impression he was a fool, but if he were, that would explain a lot. In more civilized regions authorities have grown increasingly skeptical of men who obey homicidal voices. Surely countless theologians have pondered what lessons can be learned from a deity who rewards a father for his willingness to slay his son. Still, the legacy endured. From Abraham the patriarch sprang the pattern of Western faith, the covenant sealed in violence on Mount Moriah, and I was the currency.

You could say I was foolishly self-absorbed in a matter that, after all, affected us all, but *I* was the one who'd been bound up for slaughter. I can still feel the iron, filicidal blade poised on my submissive throat. Yet my memory may have been corrupted by the story as told in Genesis. We'd spent three exhausting days ascending the slope in searing sun, my father and I. I was older than is generally believed, somewhere in my twenties. I could have overpowered him. We were all knife men in that desert. I was frightened, yes, but it wasn't fear that made me so obliging. It was disbelief. The ram that eventually took my place had more sense. He struggled.

CHAPTER 6

RUTH

Borges left two messages, neither very detailed. He was staying in the same posh little hotel on the beach in Santa Monica where we'd spotted Jordan's Queen Noor in the elevator. To screen out rabble and make guests feel even more exclusive, it had no sign out front. There were paintings in the lobby you could trade for a chalet in St. Moritz.

I didn't call him back, but when he tried a third time I picked up.

"Look," he said, "I'm sorry I haven't called."

"I didn't want you to."

"But it's been a year."

"Who's counting?"

He gave me the laugh I suppose I'd been seeking. "No one catches you speechless, do they?" He explained he was in town for a short stay and invited me to lunch, claiming he wanted to discuss my dissertation.

"You read it?"

"Yes, it was brilliant."

"Where'd you even find it?"

"Let's talk over lunch. The restaurant next to the lobby. Remember?"

"I'm awfully busy today."

"It's just lunch, Ruth."

I was about to lose my job for the following semester because I'd stood up to a lazy, conniving student in a situation so painful I can't bear to relate the details. It involved the English Department chairman ordering me out of his office while the student looked on in delight. Experience had taught the chairman that a tenacious student with an imaginary griev-ance and only a passing interest in her classes carried far dead-lier arrows in her quiver than a pathetic freeway flyer like me. The increasing power of such students at mediocre universities and the corresponding impotence of faculty that must deal with them is an eight-hundred-pound gorilla that's rarely dis-cussed beyond the boundaries of the campuses affected. This particular chairman was an authentic loon who wore a mili-tary fatigue cap everywhere, even inside his office. Sometimes tenured professors like to parade their fantasies, and this one yearned to be Fidel Castro. He was like one of those cartoon crackpots who thought they were Napoleon. But he knew his job, which was to keep his domain uneventful.

The chairman, by the way, did look remarkably like the fifty-year-old version of Fidel, including the wispy beard and the know-it-all look of your standard egomaniac. When I first heard him speak I was shocked to hear unaccented English, which broke the spell. But putting aside his Castrophilia, he neither knew nor cared about the mediocre work of the stu-dent whose grade I refused to inflate. He just wanted me to surrender to her and make his life easier, although naturally he didn't spell that out. "If she feels that strongly about this," he said, "maybe she has a point."

"Mussolini felt strongly about things too," I reminded him. And just as those words left my mouth the student walked straight into his office without an appointment, without even knocking. Fidel instantly asked *me* to leave, sealing my fate. Now he'd have to drop me from the schedule in order to rid himself of the witness to his own shame. Understanding this at once, I burst into tears. The student beamed. When I closed the door behind me I felt myself tumbling down Alice's rabbit hole.

❖

I couldn't see how Borges, who taught at an institution too lofty to acknowledge that rabble like me even existed, could be of any help. But all the experts said you were supposed to "network" and at that juncture it would have been particularly imprudent to ignore their commandment. I'd been teaching all six of my classes (a brutal load) at one campus that semester. Now that I was on the wrong side of the *comandante* I'd have to hit the freeways again, snagging stray courses wherever I could for gravedigger wages.

I agreed to meet Borges a few blocks from his hotel at a big delicatessen on the Promenade. Lots of tables, no beds. For some reason I no longer recall, I was actually dressed up a bit that day. So I switched into jeans and a blue work shirt. But then I decided he might interpret this as date attire, so I changed back again, making me a few minutes late.

Standing near the hostess pulpit, Borges (he pronounced it "bore-jes") still exuded the kind of confidence that made you want to know him or murder him. A six-foot-four gorgeous hunk with wavy, dark blond hair that trailed down the middle of his back, broad, swimmer's shoulders, and a tendency to lean back from the waist because he was too cool for standard posture. He wore jeans with sharp creases in them, a rough cotton shirt without collar or color, red tennis shoes, and a necklace and bracelet of seashells. His unfathomable hipster-gypsy appearance was clearly intended to put you off the trail, so you'd be shocked to learn he was a professor at Dartmouth. At least that's what I thought he was. He startled me with a kiss full on the mouth, and as we waited for a table informed me he'd left Dartmouth to take a dean's position at Columbia University. On the fly, he chose his words precisely in a torrent of flawless sentences. You could find the paragraph breaks. He said he wanted to run an idea past me and that it involved something that "might be worked out" for me. At some point he began lazily caressing my arm just above the elbow. I shook him off and started for the door.

"Ruth!" He wasn't afraid to shout in public. "Ruth, please."

I turned around. "Hands to yourself, got it?"

"It's just lunch."

"Got it?"

"Got it."

"You're sure."

"Hope to die." I let him escort me back from the glass door entrance, but that upset me too.

"How dare you touch me while you're dangling a job in front of me? What are you? Some kind of moron?"

All this was overheard by the hostess and a dozen or so people waiting for tables, making it a game of verbal chicken.

"I'm sorry I was personal, but I thought we had a personal relationship. I also want to discuss an employment opportunity. One has nothing to do with the other. If there was any ethical lapse I apologize. Humbly and truly."

"You know there was. Now tell me about the job. No, wait, why, did I stand out from the forty thousand other English Ph.D.'s wandering the streets? Particularly since I never applied for a job."

"There really are forty thousand?"

"I have no idea."

"It was your dissertation. I told you. 'Eroticism and Refractory Currents in the Life and Work of Mary Shelley.'"

"So you say. Look—"

"You're not impressed I remembered the title?"

"Everybody knows about dissertations. They don't have to be true, exactly, just defensible. I didn't have time for complications, so I found clues to sexual connotations in Mary Shelley's work. They mostly led down false trails. I just left that part vague."

He laughed. Perfect, big-bad-wolf white teeth. "You intentionally titillated your committee."

"Shelley would have understood. I was running out of time and money. Besides, vagueness works wonders with a pompous audience. They can't admit they don't know what you're talking about."

"You know, Ruth, you have the makings of the finest thesis advisor in the Western World."

At that point the hostess, an eye-catching, aspiring actor, comic, producer, something—led us to a distant booth along the window, killing eavesdroppers' hopes for more blue material. Borges spent all of ten seconds reading the extensive menu. "How's the matzah ball soup?"

"Excellent, but not enough chicken."

"Tell me, why were you so . . . direct with me?"

"About the soup?"

He dipped his chin and smiled.

"As you recall, our sleeping together had nothing to do with punishment. So please stop punishing me for it. Now, proceeding on the other track—you must know your dissertation showed stunning depth. I bet you scared the hell out of your committee. But yes, of course you had your tongue in your cheek."

"Leave my tongue out of this."

"At this point, of course. But even the poorest of devils is allowed to hope."

"You're a shit, Borges."

"I refuse to be intimidated by your own self-destructive tendencies. But disregarding the false trails, you raised some tantalizing issues pertaining to Shelley's intentions in *Frankenstein*. They demand further exploration. Obviously you should be that explorer, Ruth. You don't belong teaching freshman composition in— Where are you teaching?"

"Did you really forget? Or can't you bear to pronounce its name?"

"Both. Look, you're a scholar. A genuine fucking scholar— no double entendre intended. You need to get on with your work, and we can provide the support you deserve. Simple enough, isn't it?"

"You mean you can just parachute into a deli with an Ivy League job offer? Borges, please. It would have to go through committee, all of whose members I'd need to schmooze first. Was this position ever announced? If it was, you must have a ton of applicants. Good ones too."

"Good ones? Other people like me, you mean."

Precisely. Others whose paths were cleared by correct bloodlines, schools, teeth, and trust fund balances. I smiled in affirmation. I was being unreasonably hostile but couldn't seem to stop myself. Self-destructive tendencies. He was right about that too.

"One reason people like me get to be people like me is that we don't act surprised when good things come our way. We pretend it's only natural that someone would notice our spectacular qualities. But we're just hiding the same lousy insecurities everyone else has. Let me tell you something. I read your dissertation after a colleague whose judgment I respect referred me to your article in *PMLA*. Of course when I saw the name I made the connection, but I was also mesmerized by the quality of research, the way you think, the way you write. *That's* when I looked up your dissertation. It was thrilling. A thrilling dissertation. Do you know how rare that is? And my colleagues agreed. As for our affair last year, it had nothing to do with this. Sure, I knew you were accomplished and smart. But now I know you're brilliant."

"If my brilliance was so easy to spot, how come you were the only ones to spot it?"

"Because we're brilliant too, dummy. And I hereby rescind my request to sleep with you again. In return, you have to talk business like a *mensch*."

First matzah ball soup, now Yiddish. Maybe next he'd sing something from *Fiddler on the Roof*. "Call me conceited, but I don't see you giving up that easily, and I don't like the— There's an underlying deceit to all this. The familiarity, it's wrong. It's sordid."

He shook his head in a gesture that could be surrender, affirmation, appreciation, or all of the above. "Look, once you're situated at the university—when you reach the point where you have nothing to fear from me, then and only then—don't you think I could at least try to resuscitate our relationship? Who could blame me? Look at you."

"*After* I have nothing to fear? I don't fear you now." I was lying, of course. I feared all his powers—hierarchal, intellectual, and sexual. "Besides, I'm involved with someone."

"Tell me about him."

"Let's talk about the job."

Which he did, this suave, beautiful, New York man who piled Utopian fantasies at my feet—dreams I didn't dare dream. He wasn't, I learned now, exactly *in* the English Department, but beyond it.

"We call our little enterprise the Exploratory Task Force," he said. "Sorry about the fatuous name. It didn't come from me, I assure you, but we're stuck with it for now. Many of us do tend to be literary types, but we also have people who came up through astronomy, biology—it's quite a variety. The university doesn't even try to integrate us with standard academic disciplines. You don't stick Charlie Parker in the philharmonic. Bad for him, bad for the philharmonic. We wander where we like, academically speaking, though our campus detractors call it stumbling."

"Sounds like a think tank."

"That's how we're frequently referred to. But unlike the regulation model we actually think for a living. Most think tanks are political rest stations for one side or the other. We look for scholars who will be beholden to no one and let them go out and explore what they like. Also, we never undertake institutional projects or contract with third parties. We don't form committees or any of that other tedious baggage. Sounds too good to be true, doesn't it? But it *is* true. Which is one reason our colleagues around the university would love to see us incinerated. From time to time, our scholars, when they feel it's useful, put together a seminar, but they're not listed in the catalog. We deal with students only when *we* want to. For the most part, we're not even on campus. We maintain offices there, but when our scholars feel a need to come in, most of them use our suite at Rockefeller Center. We have generous funding from our own sources, so if you need to follow something up in Paris or Abu Dhabi or wherever, you just draw a travel advance and save your receipts. We don't get terribly bureaucratic, though we prefer you shoot my assistant an email if you plan to be away any length of time."

Let's be clear on this. Leaping over the table and humping him in the booth would have been an appropriate response. Instead I nonchalantly asked him, "If it's so important to get me into your think tank or task force or whatever it is, why didn't you contact me before you came out?"

"I was planning to reach out next month. But I had last minute business to tend to out here, and since I was in town anyway, I picked up the phone. Frankly, after I got out here, I couldn't get you out of my mind."

"What were you out to do? Sleep with me or employ me? You can't have both."

"Is it really my choice to make?"

"I'm not saying I'll sleep with you. What I am saying is that if I work for you, I'll never sleep with you."

"Again," he corrected me.

"And you forget, I'm involved with someone."

Okay, maybe I was exaggerating my relationship with Lenny. Is it possible to be authentically or definitively involved with someone after what? Six days? But I felt good saying it, and I figured it was a useful thing to say under the circumstances.

Borges stroked his chin and smiled. "It's true you'd be working for me—at first, anyway. As you pointed out, one doesn't join a faculty without taking *some* procedural measures."

"Aha."

"But our administrative budget has a bit of elasticity, thanks to our foundation grants. We could deposit you on the eleventh floor while we wait for a tenure-track position to open up. If it doesn't, we'd try to get an additional slot approved. It's been done before, particularly for a scholar who can fill a vital spot in some particular research area. I'm sure we could mount a strong case for you. But a position will open up in time. People retire, they take their midlife crises to Vermont or

Costa Rica. Our last one fled to Nepal. He never even picked up his last check. Most unprofessorial, leaving money on the table like that."

"And what would I be doing on the eleventh floor?"

"You wouldn't be a *de jure* member of the faculty. On paper you'd be administering some program that doesn't exist, while really you'd be reworking your dissertation or parts of your dissertation into a book. You're one of those fortunate scholars whose subject matter relates to the popular culture, and I have a publisher friend who loves that sort of thing. While you ruminate over Shelley, you can introduce people to the authentic Frankenstein and his monster as she imagined them. Besides, he owes me. The publisher friend, that is." He placed his elbows on the table and cradled his chin with his thumbs, watching me expectantly.

As you've no doubt gathered, Borges had been a one-night stand. I've had two, total. I was introduced to him at a chic party at a Palos Verdes mansion. I'd tagged along with a friend. Every woman there noticed the tall, sexy, academic celebrity in a suit they tell me was Armani. How people who aren't haberdashers recognize one brand of suit from another I haven't a clue. Can't they fill their heads with more critical data? How to identify poison mushrooms, for example.

Even in that gathering of intellectual and show-biz celebrities Borges was a star. I met him moments after watching Ariana Huffington practically fellate him so he'd "do something" for her website. He'd moderated a UCLA panel discussion that afternoon that included Don DeLillo and Philip Roth. His Saul Bellow biography had won a Pulitzer. Now it was a best seller all over again after a boost from Oprah.

Not long after Borges and I began swapping flirtatious observations, Drew Barrymore inserted herself between us wearing a dress that left a nipple exposed to the elements. She ignored me while explaining at length why "everything happens for a reason." But eventually she and her nipple ambled off with the host, the elegant Deepak Chopra, who later headed off an ugly incident involving Borges and a famous prizefighter. This wasn't Deepak Chopra the fabulously successful self-help guru who advocates spirituality to deal with illness, but another Deepak Chopra, a tech tycoon. He'd built his palace on a bluff above the beach with a sweeping view of the L.A. coastline all the way to Malibu. The house was a mix of architectural styles, like a sandwich with everything on it. Out front stood an artificial waterfall and two statues of maharajas atop elephants. You could have opened the living room to a herd of elephants and still had room for a miniature golf course.

I remember looking at the rare paintings and sculptures, the exquisite furnishings, and thinking how much more precious would be something, anything, left from my life before that night at the carnival. The sociocrats in charge had trashed my heirlooms without stopping to consider I'd grow into an adult hungry for answers. If they'd saved a hairpin, a ribbon, a shoelace, I'd have treated it like a stack of Picassos.

◆

The prizefighter was a champion or ex-champion—I don't really know which—who'd been involved in a series of scrapes with the law, not all of them minor. Shortly after Chopra steered Barrymore away, I took a bathroom break and returned to find Borges and the fighter close enough to dance. They were surrounded by a circle of gaping onlookers, all keeping a respectful distance. The fighter, clearly crazy, was shouting, "You double-crossed me!" and other words to that effect, including "dirty motherfucker," "cocksucking motherfucker," and several other subcategories of motherfucker. I thought it must be a case of mistaken identity. How could an academic star double-cross a boxer? The boxer—a heavyweight, no less— was accompanied by another giant who was also purple angry.

Neither had a neck. Their heads were like giant brown pumpkins growing straight out of their shoulders. Someone said that the second man was, unbelievably, the fighter's bodyguard.

"Why in God's name does a big nasty boxing champion need a bodyguard?" I asked an untroubled man in penny loafers who, I'd been told, was once a boxing columnist. He was also a minor novelist. Ivan something. Goldberg, I think.

The bodyguard wasn't there to protect the fighter, Goldberg explained. The fighter, whose name was Billy Blankenship, had him on his payroll to keep *himself* from hurting or killing someone. "Also to pull groupies off him. They're like octopuses sometimes."

"I've met octopuses. They weren't female."

"Am I supposed to apologize for every jerk guy you ever met? I don't blame you for Leni Riefenstahl, do I?"

"You dated Leni Riefenstahl? You don't look *that* old."

"Ouch. Let me tell you something about Leni Riefenstahl. You know who finally arrested her? A boxing writer. Budd Schulberg. Who was also a novelist and—"

"—a screenwriter," I said. "He wrote—"

"*On the Waterfront*," we said in unison, followed by appreciative smiles.

"Schulberg was a Navy officer in the OSS," Goldberg said. "After Germany surrendered he found Riefenstahl and took her to jail in Nuremburg."

"Oddly enough, Ivan, I find that interesting. But—"

"Why oddly? It *is* interesting."

"Right, but I was going to say . . . somebody might be killed here any minute."

"I know. I was working up the nerve to slide in there and separate them. Fighters don't hit boxing writers. That's a rule. The bodyguard could be a problem though. Chatting with you seemed safer." He looked me up and down as though I were an art object and added, "Or maybe not."

"Cute," I said.

"Who, me?"

"No, clearly you're a bastard. But what you *say* is cute. Sometimes."

The tension had reached an unsustainable intensity, yet Borges never stopped grinning. He was absolutely calm and fearless. In fact, he was clearly struggling not to laugh in the face of Blankenship, who was no longer calling him names but appeared to be deciding which of his features to crush first. The fighter's stare was so utterly fierce and terrifying I wondered how his opponents could stand it. It kept us rooted to the floor, helpless.

"Let's assume your assessment is entirely correct," Borges told him. "Even so, please, have some sympathy. And—" here he paused, "—some taste." At that point Borges lost control and exploded into laughter. I closed my eyes, expecting thuds, gasps, screams, sirens. When I heard none of that I peered into the circle again and saw Blankenship grimacing as though shot with an arrow. Something had transformed him into a timid, apologetic creature flashing Borges a sickly smile. It was all terribly baffling. About this time Chopra showed up and convinced the two of them to shake hands.

Before Goldberg drifted off to look for his wife I asked him for the number of his agent. Even then I secretly toyed with the idea of writing a modern intellectual history using Shelley as my centerpiece.

"My agent?" he said, "I call him the albatross. If it turns out I don't like you, I'll give you his number."

I made a mental note to find one of Goldberg's books, but I never got around to it. I never got his agent's number either.

When I asked Borges what had sparked his quarrel with Blankenship, he scratched his ear a bit before saying it was a confidential matter. "And not," he added, "a terribly important one."

This was right around the time I was gradually breaking free of Skip. And there I was surrounded by the storybook extravagance of Chopra's mansion, which, let's face it, was a kind of aphrodisiac. At the same time I was presented with

Borges, a man who was industrial-strength charming, now a nonviolent superhero as well, who'd passed up at least one nipple-baring starlet to woo me. When we kissed on the dance floor I decided that someone I'd never see again was precisely what I could use off the evening menu. And when he called a year later I had no intention of renewing our "affair," as he called it.

◆

The *PMLA* article that delighted Borges had precisely the reverse effect on my employers, who, upon its publication, treated me with even greater helpings of the fear and loathing Hunter Thompson detected in so many dark corners of America. I realized then that if I did one more thing right I'd be out of a job. Refusing to give in to the conniving student was that thing. And now in this deli it appeared I'd stumbled into a miracle. Like one of those people who brings home a dusty old frame from a flea market and finds a long-lost Wyeth beneath the photo. People win Rhodes Scholarships and bump into perfect love with their grocery carts. Maybe it was my turn.

I devoured a corned beef sandwich that was big as a steam iron, and as I waited for Borges to finish his soup I treated myself to a waking dream that included the pangs and pleasures of a bicoastal romance with Lenny. Breaking through clouds of ecstasy, I strafed the *comandante* with fifty-caliber ordnance and soared off to my sweet Lenny and a spot at a real university where Borges, presiding over an impregnable enclave, protected me from the wicked and the witless. How could he begin to understand the power of such a promise to a foster child? We're on our own after our eighteenth birthday, one step ahead of a cardboard box on the street. When I was going to school, just having a place to go between semesters would have been heaven. Frost said home is the place where, when you have to go there, they have to take you in. No such place had ever existed for me.

LENNY

"This is important, isn't it?" I blurted out.

"Important?" Spotting trouble, she was instantly alert.

"Important, life-changing, momentous. Something that—
You describe it then." We'd just finished a delicious round of
love. I was nestled inside her, and my emotions, my deeply
human desire to have it all verified, ran free.

"No," she said, clinging to my neck. "No." She buried
her face in my chest and squeezed me tight. When she pulled
back I spotted a tear born of contentment, hope, glee, and, I
thought, a dash of despair. Who could blame her? This Dick-
ensian outcast with urchin eyes (one eyebrow raised just a tad)
and the practiced nostrils of a consecutively swindled child.
And there I was lying to her. It wasn't deliberate. Our close-
ness had fooled me into thinking of myself as a regulation
mortal. Now I'd made everything worse for both of us. She
thought it was too early to discuss our future. It wasn't early.
We had no future, so we were near the end. And it was so
terribly hard, like leaving a comrade on the battlefield.

I marveled at my idiocy. At that point I'd spent seven
days with Ruth. Okay, three more, tops. No more excuses.
But after she left to teach a couple of classes I found myself
not just missing her, but *nostalgic* for her, for the look and
feel of her, the brave smile and tender delight that overcame
the mountain of logic telling her to ease up. Well one ruined
Tamara was all I could stand per lifetime, even if that lifetime
was measured by its own peculiar clock.

We were two of a kind, Ruth and I. Is a parent who ditches
you at a carnival more or less lamentable than a father perfectly

receptive to cutting your throat, actually *planning* it, in fact, like just another chore? Which was more depraved? Drowning the puppy or throwing it out along the highway?

After I let her go without explanation and she had time to think it over, how could she possibly miss a reprehensible lout like me?

CHAPTER 7

RUTH

A confused mini-moment—a leap from an instantly forgotten dream, an unsettling one—into wakefulness. Evelyn was gently but tenaciously shaking my shoulder. I found myself stretched out on the sofa in yesterday's work clothes. A CNN news reader spoke of turmoil in Pakistan, his voice exuding practiced concern. I looked at the screen and it showed angry people in the street. But it was impossible to know precisely how the images related to the voice-over or whether the footage was even current. The important thing was to keep viewers involved, as though we were all infants attracted to bright colors.

The bathroom mirror showed matted, dirty hair like yesterday only dirtier. God, I taught two classes looking like this. Should have worn a hat.

The shower refreshed me, but not as much as I'd hoped. It was time. First I carefully laid out some clothes. Mustn't do this in a ratty robe. Minutes later, cleaned and dressed, I sat down at the kitchen table, phone in hand. Evelyn came over and brushed some hairs off my forehead. "One last question. This guy in New York, is he trouble too?"

"Minor trouble, I expect."

"Beauties and their troubles. I should have such troubles."

I'd taken two or three phone calls from Borges's functionaries, who were already talking salary. Unless this was some kind of diabolical conspiracy involving a squad of professional actors, further suspicion was unwarranted. The offer was genuine.

Evelyn left the room as I punched in Lenny's number. "Hello?" Crap! It was him, no message, and . . . Where was it in my head, what I planned to say? Nearly hung up in terror, but how juvenile was that? All these damn cell phones have caller ID. I closed my eyes and fished words from my frozen brain, rushing ahead like I was reading a communiqué . . . Jesus, I was shouting, probably in some misguided belief it would prevent my voice from quavering. "You have to tell me why you're avoiding me. This isn't high school. I thought—" But I lost my place, couldn't find any more of what I'd rehearsed in my head . . . sticky silence . . . "I thought we had . . . something, Lenny. Please tell me, explain it to me. I'm not stalking you, but I need to know what— You have to tell me why, understand? You have to."

LENNY

A horse hitched to a wagon was collapsed in the mud. A crowd watched the driver lash the animal, lying on its side, legs stretched out, eyes open, calm as a Zen priest. The horse was resigned to the lash, the owner's cruelty and its own impending death. Determined to quit the man and the misery, it didn't even bother to look at the angry, revolting figure wielding the whip but stared off into private thoughts. The closest thing I've seen to animal suicide.

The raggedy wagoner wore a workman's cap too big for him, obscuring much of his face. The crowd was strangely mute, watching with mixed horror and curiosity as the dying creature found dignity at last. Eventually I got a good look at the man's face. Mine. A phone rang. Without thinking, I answered it. And of course it was Ruth, distraught, wounded, but determined, her voice a fierce wind.

"You're right," I told her. "I know you're right, but I have to go to work, and I'm late. I'll call you back."

"When?"

Her directness and bravery made me prize her even more. And suffer more. Everything fine I'd sensed about her had proved true. I was a jackal that didn't deserve to breathe.

That morning in the library I put off what little work I had to do. I doodled her name a dozen ways. Anyone trying to talk to me had to repeat everything. Our inventory was mostly esoteric collections of papers and rare books, and we never had more than a light sprinkle of patrons, almost all of whom were professors or graduate students. How institutions like ours supported themselves mystified me. Maybe we were all CIA subsidiaries.

Running an errand to the second floor, I was so enervated I waited for the pokey elevator. My mission was to bring back a meaningless letter written by Rutherford Hayes for a Ph.D. candidate at USC who wasn't so young anymore. He was on his last extension to submit a finished dissertation and not even close to the finish, standing frozen as his future blew past him. There were many like him. I'd try to buck them up, but their minds built a relatively small task into something insurmountable. I wondered where they went off to after running out the clock. Maybe they were better off. A screwy vocation, college instructor. It didn't seem to be working out for Ruth.

The drudge seeking the Hayes letter looked so perfectly nondescript he could pull a bank job without anyone remembering the slightest thing about him. I lived in Chicago during the sixties, when academics dressed like roofers and plumbers, or at least like Marxist academics trying to look like roofers and plumbers, all hair and flannel and threadbare denim. Now they dressed like ciphers, like Scrabble blanks. Americans went to dinner in the same clothes they'd wear to the Department of Motor Vehicles. Their society was veering closer to the future that so many science fiction writers imagined, with everyone in uniform.

I needed a new location, another country to shake me up and keep my mind occupied, but taking on a new identity had become more difficult after the Twin Towers came down. Forged documents were more expensive and less reliable. Particularly in the Western democracies, bribery was riskier. Eventually I'd have to settle in some backward region. Well, I'd gone without flush toilets before.

I cleaned up my workstation for the middle-aged ex-Jesuit covering the next shift. He was always five to ten minutes early. We asked each other how we were and as usual gave positive responses without regard for the truth. I think he lived a terribly solitary life, like mine in some ways. I noticed he was making his way through *Ulysses*. If he was really determined to read novels in which nothing happened, his time might be better spent with Proust, but my ideas about time could be skewed by my exceptional situation.

On my way out I spotted The Beast coming in the door. I turned and ran out the back, my employee ID dangling from my neck.

◈

I'd grown weary of trying to analyze my perennial, predictable, and always ridiculous response to a Beast sighting. Besides, I was too busy thinking about Ruth to worry about him now. In fact, five minutes later I forgot all about him. To get my mind off her I set out that night to hear some jazz, but when I got to Pamela's I had to endure a quartet led by a young, Asian-American devotee of the late John Coltrane. And like the floundering genius toward the end of his career, he was forcing a desperate train of random discord through his saxophone and pretending the calamitous outcome was marvelously cool.

"So," Jubal asked me, "you see that woman again?" Rather than construct an unsupportable tangle of lies, I'd covered myself with an easier lie, telling him that she'd lost interest.

"You know what one wrong note is?" I asked him.

"You tell me."

"A wrong note. You know what two wrong notes are?"

"Jazz," he said.

"When you know the punch line, you shouldn't play along," I said.

"That's what you get for answering a question with a question. I asked you about that professor babe, remember? Besides, I thought you dig jazz."

"I dig women, too. That doesn't mean I want to hook up with Rosie O'Donnell. Your sax man sounds like a trapped animal."

"It's challenging, what you're hearing. You may be right. Maybe we oughta smooth it out, run everything through a computer program. Like Photoshop the sound of his sax, sharpen the contrast, make the blues bluer . . . make everything easy for you. Throw in some violins and the Mormon Tabernacle Choir. Would you like that, gray boy?"

"Asshole," I said. I loved the guy.

"At last. A thoughtful retort."

"I don't like your sax man, and I'm not ashamed to say it."

"Know what your problem is?"

"What do you know about my problems?"

"You got lady problems, is what you got. So you malign a hard-working artist. They got a name for that. Know what it is?"

"Good taste?"

"Redirection of aggression. An old girlfriend taught me that. It's a deficient coping mechanism, she told me. There are much better ways to deal with your problems. For instance, you know all a those beer commercials where they show a joint full of fine ladies sitting there all alone? Just waiting to meet some guy who drinks the same brand of beer?"

I nodded. "What's your point?"

"Sure, they're bogus bars. No ugly people, no sorry-ass drunks watching daytime TV. But the fine ladies? They're real, understand? They live right here in L.A. 'cause this is where they *make* the commercials. So, my man, what you gotta do is forget your professor babe and go out and get yourself one or two a those ladies."

"I like the women in soap commercials better. The ones in beer commercials make me nervous."

"Soap commercial ladies, they got a nice way about them, but they got no bosoms and they're too involved with laundry whiteners."

"But they don't *really* care about whiteners. They're actresses."

"Yeah," he said, "but I can't fantasize about ladies who even *pretend* to go ape-shit over laundry."

"That's because you've got no imagination."

"Well, I like the ones who pretend to get frantic about beer better than the ones who pretend to get frantic about whiter laundry."

"Okay, invite them to come around. I'm not the recreation director around here."

"We get the more cerebral types. You know that."

"There's no law that says cerebral types have to look like Ernest Borgnine."

"The ladies here don't all look like Ernest Borgnine," he said. "Some of 'em look like Al Sharpton."

Jubal, except for a gap between his front teeth, looked like a younger Sidney Poitier. Yet he never struck me as conceited. We related like contemporaries even though he was barely forty. I used to wonder why such companionships felt natural to me. But as they get older, people often describe themselves as exactly the same person they always were. Only the exterior keeps changing, and it's that exterior that defines them to everyone else. Ultimately, I suppose they're trapped in the wrong body, which is perhaps why I thought I was living in precisely the correct body.

Long ago I used to watch myself for signs of aging. After all, my condition came with no guarantees. Was my skin wrinkling at last? My hair thinning? A varicose vein forming on my calf? But eventually, like a child of wealth, I took my status for granted. Individual temperament is like a warm-blooded body that reverts to its proper temperature. That's why, according to a phantom study, winners of lotteries and victims of horrendous car crashes are equally content several months later.

I'd met Jubal almost a year earlier. Zev had asked me to accompany a celebrated boxing promoter to Las Vegas where he was negotiating a contract with another promoter. They'd taken a break and wouldn't resume for hours, so while the promoter napped in his room I was free to nurse a tonic and lime at the casino showroom. I recall the graceful Vegas showgirls unsexed by the hideous, altitudinous contraptions they had to balance atop their heads, the rhinestone-and-feather-encrusted phallic towers that turned gorgeous, long-legged women into awkward creatures who couldn't inspire an erection in a P.O.W. camp. I could never figure out whether the costume designers were playing an elaborate prank or were actually in earnest.

A young black man wearing dark glasses and with a cell phone to his ear had stopped in front of my little table, partially blocking my view of the neutered amazons. "Wait, wait, let me take it down," he shouted, oblivious to the stage show behind him. After frantically searching his pockets he asked me for a pen, forming a tent with his fingertips. I handed him one. Only rarely can you catch me without a pen, a pocket knife or a handkerchief. He scrawled a series of numbers on what looked like a parking stub. Competing with the show music, he yelled into the phone, giving assurances, reciting pieces of his schedule. A tuxedoed maître d' across the room shook his head and headed over.

"Right, right, right," the talker said. "Listen, I really gotta go, okay? I'll call you with the information." He closed his phone and the maître d', a tall Hispanic, moved on without a word. The talker jotted something more on the stub and looked at me. "I just came from Barbados. I got some people want to build a sound stage there. You know the Time Warner Building?"

"In New York?"

"Yeah, these people I'm with, they're trying to do a deal on that too. There's this guy wants to buy it. I tell him it's a billion dollars. He says, 'Sounds ball-parky.' That's how this guy talks. There was another guy trying to buy it too, but he wasn't nearly as amusing."

He spoke the way whirling dervishes moved. In a society where physicians endorse penis-enlargement pills, Jubal's tales would have to be classified as relatively reliable. I'd guess he knew people who *wanted* to buy the Time Warner Building, though I'm not sure they could muster financing for one of the taxis waiting outside the entrance.

"I gotta get back to Barbados next week. Lookit."

He pulled out a brown leather wallet and showed me some sort of non-U.S. currency. "I got nothing but Barbados dollars and chits from a stripper bar." I invited him to sit down. "Can't. My lady's waiting at a baccarat table. But hey, if there's anything I can do for you—"

"You can give me back my pen."

We traded names and established we both lived in L.A. Not an unusual occurrence in Vegas.

"Look, my lady? She owns a joint on Wilshire. It's called Pamela's. Jazz every night. Come by, okay? I'll buy you one."

"Wilshire's a big street."

"At Seventh Street, man. In Santa Monica." Though I'm wary of making friends, I've always enjoyed being around people. That's how I came to be in the Farmers Market food court the day I met Ruth. And despite myself, I became Jubal's friend.

❖

There's a façade to The Beast, a papier-maché quality to his phantom presence that's like the world's most obvious toupee, except no one can recognize it but me. He was stepping up his appearances. The library sighting was the third in less than a hundred years, signifying something. He had an entire world to roam, but clearly he had some level of interest in me, in detritus, a freak created for a reason long since forgotten.

Set in the context of all I'd seen and done, my feelings for Ruth were a ridiculous luxury. Much of my life I worked like a dog just trying to keep myself fed and clothed. The earth has not been all that hospitable to most folks. Tamara once had to sit still while I dug a tooth from her mouth with a knife. I cried as I worked. She comforted me as blood ran down her chin.

When I've lived in places where life should have been easy it was made difficult anyway by the congenital lunacy of the species. I recall a land with mild winters where you could scoop fish from the lake with an urn. I'm not sure where it was or when. I don't think I lived there very long. I can't even identify the language we spoke. What I do remember is that more time on their hands brought no paradise to residents. It gave them the leisure to scheme and slay one another over useless possessions or their dueling gods and mythologies. Where living should have been more relaxed, the fog of death was particularly thick. The warriors, as always, were barely beyond puberty. My father's willingness to spend my young life has been, down through time, persistently mimicked by kings quick to squander the youths in their care. Both the Israeli army and the U.S. Marines—two of the most proficient military forces on earth—prefer recruits no older than eighteen, before their spirit of sacrifice has a chance to be tempered with cold reasoning.

If The Beast had business with me, leaving L.A. wouldn't help. But his presence gave me added incentive to flee Ruth. If you're about to be run over by a bus, you don't want to be holding the hand of someone you care about.

I spent the next day working the sidelines at a USC football game, making sure drunks didn't run onto the field, one of their rituals. American football mystifies me, creating such profuse passion as a few minutes of organized mayhem are strung out over three and a half hours.

After the game, weary from too much sun, I inched out of the lot with thousands of other vehicles and crawled along the freeway for miles. When I finally exited a few blocks from home, a stoplight turned green and the SUV hulk in front of me failed to move. I banged the horn and a split second later spotted a caretaker shepherding a file of innocents across the path of the SUV, which had hidden them from view. All had, in the parlance of the day, special needs—a pair of teens with Down syndrome, a young woman with a specialized cane in each hand working like the devil to maneuver her terribly bent legs, a blind man, and so forth. A regular Fellini parade. If they'd shaken their fists at me I might have found my offense easier to bear. But they smiled, seeking my forgiveness as they limped toward a future of more dolts like me.

Regrets can be impossible to bear just in the course of a standard lifetime. In my case a pyramid of self-reproach had been building stone by stone on my chest for forty centuries. This was a new sorrow to crush me at unpredictable moments. A small yellow sign only a few feet from where I waited advertised "Real Estate Millionaires Share Their Secrets," followed by a phone number. A grandiose claim for a humble sign nailed to a stick in the ground. I tried to picture real estate millionaires pouring out their secrets to curious callers and wondered anew just where our species was headed, where I was headed. The driver behind me honked. I was holding up traffic.

Pulling up to the driveway at last, I found Ruth leaning against her truck.

CHAPTER 8

RUTH

For a moment I told myself everything would be okay, but then I saw his face was like a vacant billboard and I felt my insides collapse. What had I been thinking? If not paralyzed by nausea I might have turned and run. Fortunately there were two sidewalk yuppies who stopped in front of me to admire each other's dogs. As he moved around them it gave the vapor in my mind time to settle. So though my voice shook I began telling him about Skip, pretty much the way I'd rehearsed it to myself: "I used to tell him, 'Skip, when someone says goodbye, you say goodbye and hang up. You don't just dribble out more conversation. You know how I hate that.' But it's what he did over and over and finally I'd just say, 'Gotta go.' Click. I never thought I'd turn into another Skip, but—" I felt so clumsy I just shut it down and gazed at my shoes. God, I was pathetic.

"It's not your fault," he said softly. "I don't deserve you." When I looked up, his face was familiar again, but tortured.

I walked straight up to him, almost nose to nose. "What the fuck is going on?" I said.

He managed a smile, and I smiled back, but not for long. He leaned forward to kiss me, no hands. I stepped back.

"I'm moving to New York," I told him.

He weighed the information, but I couldn't discern its impact. "What will you do there?"

"I'll be at Columbia."

"University," he said, as though I might mean Columbia Widget Distributors or Columbia Trash Hauling.

"I couldn't even get arrested in L.A." He nodded. Somehow this perfectly honest conversation had degenerated into mannered mush. "Wait a minute," I said. "Let's cut the bullshit. What's going on? I *know* how you feel, Lenny. I know it."

"I didn't call because I didn't want to lie to you."

"What lies have you told already? You're married, right?"

"It can't work, Ruth. It just won't."

I was getting dropped off at the carnival all over again. My parents never told me why either.

"I don't stand talking in the wind," I said.

"What wind? There's no wind."

"From *The Searchers*. John Wayne said it so Chief Scar would let him into his teepee."

He looked at me wistfully, as though I were a stream he couldn't cross.

"Look me in the eye," I said. "Okay, are you or are you not married?"

He waited a moment, then shook his head no.

"Why not blurt it out? Whatever it is?"

"That wouldn't work either."

"Was it something I said? Something I did? Something I am?"

"You didn't do anything, Ruth. I mean anything wrong. That's part of the problem."

"What's the other part?"

"You're going to New York when?"

"New York's not the problem. It was— I just used it as an excuse to see you."

"You hungry?"

"No. Yes. Wait a minute. We're talking bullshit again."

"Look, when *are* you going to New York?"

"Two weeks maybe."

"Don't cry," he said.

"You act sweet, then cruel, then sweet again," I said through tears. "I can't stand it, Lenny."

I let him put his arms around me. He had hot dog breath. I loved it. I burrowed my head into his shoulder, rubbing tears on his shirt.

"I'll try to stay sweet then, but when you get to New York, forget me. Can you do that?"

I broke away. I wasn't so much angry, just fierce. "Can you forget *me*?" I asked him.

"I don't talk standing in the wind."

"You mean you don't stand talking in the wind."

"That too. I've got nothing to eat in there but canned tuna and Oreo cookies."

I let out a deep breath. I must have forgotten to breathe for a while. "Sold," I said.

LENNY

"It's not going to work," she said as I closed the door behind us. "I can't do sex, not with all this weirdness and mystery hanging over us. We'd both be whores."

I took her purse and placed it on a chair. "Then let's just be pals."

"Don't make fun of me."

"I wasn't, I don't think. I mean . . . I meant it. Maybe it came out wrong."

She watched my face, deciding. "Then let's go out for real food," she said finally.

"Can you make it to Santa Monica or are you too hungry?"

She grabbed a stale Oreo for the trip, and we headed for Pamela's. I guess I wanted to show her off. All the way over I felt alternating waves of delight and regret, fire and ice. I longed for a tomorrow that could never be. I asked nothing about her new job, the 401(k), or any other twenty-first century trivia. But if I thought about it, I'd have been pleased for her. Columbia. That had to be good. Sometimes the righteous reap rewards.

◆

Neither of us was terribly adept at pretending everything was coming up roses. Pam liked her anyway, and of course Jubal told me she was a knockout, though I knew she was a bit thin for his tastes. Pam was twenty or thirty pounds north of *Vogue* territory and quite comfortable in her own skin, always dealing cheerfully with sales people, musicians, customers, and the hundred little chores she saw to each day. As she and Jubal drew closer he'd gradually toned down his raps, was not so interruptive and more likely to think before he spoke. Pamela was the proverbial good woman who, by example, was shaping him into a better man. Not for the first time I thought how lovely it must be to grow old with someone you care about, your mutual tenderness multiplying as gray hairs and random aches and pains escort you toward the finish.

A trio played West Coast cool as Ruth and I ate tasty salads and pasta. When we got back to my place we fucked our teeth loose.

CHAPTER 9

LENNY

Ruth was out before six, brushing my lips with hers and leaving without a word. That should have been welcome to me, but it was unsettling. That was the conundrum. I wanted her to go on with her life undamaged, but if she were to forget me I'd be crushed. I could distinguish sweet from sad, pleasure from pain, right from wrong, but it was no use. Desire and selfishness crushed all. In the context of our situation, I couldn't even say what it was I really wanted from Ruth. Love and a normal life? That wasn't even possible. What I'd always had instead was time—time that's supposed to heal all wounds and perhaps bring a share of wisdom. We'd just take whatever we could from our remaining time together, Ruth and I. Meanwhile I'd go about my business within the confines of my freakish life, Beast or no Beast.

I had another assignment that morning with the boxing promoter, accompanying him to a graveside funeral service up in the valley. The deceased had been a celebrity once, a feared heavyweight champion. But though beaten into retirement, Billy Blankenship hadn't disappeared from public view entirely. He'd drive head-on into a tree or throw a paparazzo over a fence, extending his fame beyond fifteen minutes. Now he'd made the news one last time by sticking a pistol in his mouth and pulling the trigger.

It was a typical L.A. morning—no weather to speak of—a light breeze, low humidity, just enough warmth to have no effect on the senses. But as soon as the limo crossed the Santa Monica Ridge the sunlight took on a desert harshness that made shade more precious. It was a graveside service. Were it not for the fighter's eight or nine children and their assorted mothers, there'd have been practically no one at all.

The three TV crews were clearly disappointed to find no treasure trove of celebrities, so they centered their stories on the low turnout. "With few friends or fans left, Billy Blankenship made a lonely, violent exit," pronounced one reporter, loud enough for the fighter's children to hear, and she was doing more than one take. The promoter, Ray Powell, told me to shut her up. I found that a reasonable request and made a deal with her producer, finding the crew a spot that was out of earshot yet afforded a cleaner camera angle. I preferred to do my job tactfully, and so did our clients, except for occasional oddballs who liked to pretend they were Sonny Corleone.

Defusing situations was my specialty and the principal reason Zev employed me. My peacemaking ability is the closest thing I have to a supernatural power. I'd seen so much senseless violence over time that I could recognize its contours from a distance and devise blood-free solutions to head it off—even as it called to me, as it does to all of us. Fondness for bloodshed has no geographic or epochal boundaries. It's one of those inherent human conditions like tribalism, love, jealousy, or staring into campfires.

The minister was tied up in traffic. While we waited, Powell, the only celebrity to be found, waltzed through three consecutive TV interviews, smooth, unruffled, cutting each reporter off after ninety seconds. "They use only thirty, maybe sixty seconds tops for one talking head," he explained. "You let them shoot too much footage, they can edit out your message. Gives them too much power."

Powell was a dapper, slim, black man in his seventies who moved like someone thirty years younger. In a business that held out few rewards for moral sensitivity, he was a particularly effective player who'd gradually elbowed most of his top competitors off the playing field. He claimed he'd mastered the principles of business from Machiavelli and other great thinkers he'd studied in the prison library while doing a four-year stretch for manslaughter. Glorying in media attention was one of his few addictions, and in each of his three camera sessions he easily articulated a precisely calibrated measure of sorrow and praise. "A terrible loss, just horrific for everyone. I wish Billy had come to me with his problems." It was well-known that Powell *was* a Blankenship problem, having sliced open his financial belly with the finesse of a five-star sushi chef. But none of the reporters, even if they were aware of it, raised the issue.

A lesser celebrity, a ruthless fixer and hedge fund manager named Trianon, showed up later with two blondes in little black dresses. He smiled for the camera but shook off interview requests. I recalled reading that when Blankenship was champion, Trianon had given him some financial advice and subsequently billed him for six figures. No one seemed to know whether Blankenship paid it.

"Shame about Billy," Trianon said to Powell. They shook hands, two bloodsuckers with different specialties.

Most of Zev's employees counted the Playboy Mansion as the best possible assignment, though the young women there, dismissing bodyguards as neither wealthy nor particularly well-connected, treated us like pool furniture. I much preferred the Powell assignment even though I'd learned long ago that if you want to keep a low profile, you stay away from celebrities.

Powell was an interesting character who never made ridiculous demands, unlike some of our power-hitters out of Hollywood who expected us to double as errand boys and pimps. Only recently Zev had been forced to call Las Vegas and explain to a major talent agent that he'd have to make his own companionship arrangements. He'd been demanding fresh hookers for his hotel suite like items from a catalog. "This guy says he wants Asian girls only," an exasperated co-worker told me. "And get this. They have to have big tits. What is he, nuts? You don't go to a Chinese restaurant for a BLT."

Powell, whose business often took him to Las Vegas, Atlantic City, and other fleshpots, was himself a straight arrow who rarely drank and remained, as far as I knew, faithful to his wife.

◈

The Muslim minister, a round man with caramel skin, walked directly up to Powell, collected two hundred dollar bills, found himself a good spot, and moved straight into his eulogy.

"Man's still got one camera crew left," Powell whispered to me. "Doesn't want to waste it." Though a good sixty percent of the tribute appeared to be one-size-fits-all, it was absorbing nevertheless. Near its end he read portions of a Langston Hughes poem:

> *They send me to eat in the kitchen*
> *When company comes,*
> *But I laugh,*
> *And eat well,*
> *And grow strong.*

"Billy might have thrived had he eaten at a kinder table," lamented the preacher, "but America designates another kind of table for ghetto children. They eat with the rats. Billy was tough, a tough brother who fought his way out of there, but injustice pursued him till it made him so sick and got him in the end. He's *found* his justice now. Found it at last. Finally sits at the big table. I know it. I feel it. Allah is just."

Mothers of the fighter's children sat with stoic dignity in honored, front row seats as the minister, finished with his oratory, proceeded down the line to extend condolences. Powell and Trianon took their turns tossing a shovelful of earth onto the casket. Suddenly a black man wearing gray sweats and a black baseball cap planted himself in front of Powell. An ex-fighter for sure, his head swiveled slowly in perpetual cadence,

- 90 -

left-right-left, reminding me of a snake. "You still livin' good, Ray? Bet you are, bet you livin' real good." Without waiting for a response, he drifted away like Banquo's ghost. I recall his eyes slanting down toward his earlobes, making his face look perpetually sad, almost like a caricature of a perpetually sad face, a representation of all the forgotten wretches who'd gone before him down through time, all the exploited rabble who toiled and died without ever catching a break. Meanwhile I—who'd kept my limbs and health these four thousand years, who'd tasted innumerable perfect sunrises and sunsets, took—relatively speaking—only mild pleasure in my spectacular good fortune. It was pathetic, laughable really. I'd have chuckled if I weren't at a funeral.

Another figure approached Powell, out of nowhere it seemed, tall and sturdy—The Beast, looking just as he had at the library. Two appearances in three days. Though struck by panic, I called on every fiber in my body to resist running off as I'd done for centuries. I backed up a couple of steps, then skipped forward, regaining my ground as though on a playing field. Powell and the hedge fund manager glanced at me quizzically. The three of them discussed the deceased, but I couldn't follow their words. I could barely breathe.

Powell: "What the hell was wrong with you out there, man?" We were inside the limo, back on the freeway, and I wasn't completely sure how I got there. "You're supposed to be my badass protection? You are one sorry motherfucker, you know that?"

I blinked. "May I have some water?"

"That cuts it! Abner, pull over. Let this useless motherfucker out a here. You hear me? Thinks I'm his goddamn waiter."

"I pull over on the freeway for nothing, cops won't like it, boss."

"We're doing what? Five miles an hour? It's not—"

"Mr. Powell," I broke in, "if you don't mind, who was that guy? What was his name?"

He leaned forward in the plush leather. "If I don't mind? Don't you understand you're gonna be fired? Not just by me. I will talk to Zev and he will can your ass, get it?"

"Who was he? The tall white guy talking to you before we left."

"Abner, now what you doing?"

"Getting to the exit ramp, boss."

"We don't exit here. Is everybody in this car crazy but me?"

"Thought you wanna let this guy out."

"Forget it. Get me to the office. I already wasted half the damn day on a broken-down, dead fighter."

Somehow I'd forgotten there was a drinks rack right in front of me. I pulled out a plastic water bottle and drained half.

"Anything else we can do for you, Mr.——? What the fuck's your name?"

"Lenny."

"—Mr. Lenny."

"Who was that guy?"

"None a your goddamn business is who he was."

"I thought I knew him."

Powell leaned back again and looked straight ahead. "Yeah? Well let me tell you something. He's a good man not to know."

"But—"

"Just shut up about him."

No one said another word until twenty minutes later when we pulled into the garage of his office tower in the mid-Wilshire District. We were very near the spot where RFK was murdered and history took a terrible turn. The Ambassador Hotel had already been torn down to make way for another building that wouldn't last forty years.

Powell, still looking straight ahead, asked me in the darkness, "He closing in on you?"

"Not just him."

"Yeah, it's all been closing in on me long as I can remember. Just try to stay ahead of it."

I nodded.

"If it's not too late," he added.

CHAPTER 10

*M*ary Shelley *(1797–1851), British novelist, essayist, drama-tist, and travel writer, was the daughter of two philosophers. A free-spirited thinker who would become one of the most creative novelists in the history of womankind, she finished* Frankenstein: or, The Modern Prometheus *before reaching her twentieth birthday. Years after her death, a pervasive new medium in Hol-lywood, California would mutilate her masterpiece, mercilessly gutting the metaphysical subtlety and lyricism and melting the remaining carcass into a celluloid sausage that would become her false legacy.*

Shelley's creature wasn't a grunting oaf but a self-educated, well-spoken, often well-meaning individual. But characters who encountered him invariably reacted viciously to his freakish appearance. Eventually, after learning to anticipate their brut-ishness, he turned not only melancholy, but also calculating and cruel. He blamed his brilliant creator, Victor Frankenstein, for producing a living soul that could find neither companionship nor contentment.

Frankenstein never dignified his invention with a name, referring to him as "the creature," "the fiend," "the monster," and similar appellations. The two of them engaged in a twisted waltz of violence and vengeance that sprawled over thousands of miles and hundreds of pages. Before they died, each would murder the bride of the other. But the creature didn't slay his creator and mourned the death with tears. Finally, consumed by grief, remorse, and uncompromising loneliness, Frankenstein's creation rode an ice floe to certain death into the Arctic vastness.

"I shall no longer see the sun or stars or feel the winds play on my cheeks," he said. "Light, feeling, and sense will pass away, and in this condition must I find my happiness."

—Notes for an unpublished article by Ruth Canby

RUTH

Spread out on the living room floor, I was almost finished painting my nails black to go with my high-heeled sandals. I was a whore, so I might as well look like one. Being a whore doesn't feel so bad. What feels bad is discovering you don't feel so bad about being a whore.

"I ever tell you I used to date a married man?" Evelyn asked me. "Or maybe dating isn't what you call it. What *do* you call it?"

"You were probably bored," I said. She was still convinced Lenny was married or worse, though she couldn't define "worse." She knew I was preparing to go to his place.

"You know, you're going to meet the coolest people out there. Really. You still don't realize what a great deal you're getting. I mean, you understand it, sure, but do you *realize* it? No more grading infantile essays, no more saying the same things semester after semester to all those unappreciative little shits who don't want to hear it anyway. You're on the red carpet, babe." She'd taught high school some years back and had been wounded by the experience. It was difficult to find an experience that hadn't wounded Evelyn.

Unlike her, I didn't loathe my students, not even as I slogged through stacks of essays that, for the most part, were shockingly devoid of thought or articulation. Mostly I rooted for them. I thought they were getting a raw deal because their education had been dumbed down along with so much else in America and no one seemed to have an answer for it. No matter how hard I tried I couldn't, in one semester, undo all the intellectual damage inflicted on them by the inanity of the global village that so prodigiously seduced them into semi-literacy.

"Cut it out," I told Evelyn.

"Cut what out?"

"You know—worrying." She'd be living alone again. No one to share the popcorn, no one to hear her witty comments that accompanied the dopey TV shows she was obliged to watch.

"It's not easy for me to make friends. You were an anomaly," she said.

"You're speaking of me in the past tense. God, you're a goof sometimes."

"All the time. It's part of my charm."

"Look, not that it matters anymore, but Lenny's not who— not *what* you think he is." I closed the cap on the nail polish. "Where are my keys?"

"On the microwave. Aren't you curious about what happened to my married man?"

"I figured you just nagged him to death, poor devil."

She smiled. Evelyn had a really sweet smile, and you could crack her up with good jokes or bad. She didn't belong in the humorless world of soap opera.

"Look," I asked her, "did you ever consider Lenny might have some kind of, you know, problems? Serious problems. An awful illness, or maybe he suffered a terrible calamity at some point."

"Which would you prefer? That you fell for someone with a mysterious illness? Or someone who's a miserable lying, healthy son-of-a-bitch? Don't tell me. I already know. You can be such a schlemiel. You really can."

"Jesus, Evelyn, you'd honestly wish sickness on someone?"

She tilted her head and smiled. But I knew she wasn't the tough character she pretended to be.

◆

After inviting me in, Lenny asked me where I'd like to go. He suggested a couple of restaurants.

"Shut up," I said, kicking off a shoe.

LENNY

The last days together were hard. So many topics were out of bounds. Our conversation became monosyllabic. Communication was channeled into increasingly desperate lovemaking. Then she left for New York without saying goodbye. I had it coming, but it jolted me anyway. Meanwhile Powell, no longer threatening to have me fired, had begun asking for me on a regular basis. I obliged. Maybe it would speed up whatever was going to happen between me and The Beast—a possibility I looked at with alternating dread and curiosity. Trying to prepare for him was useless. He showed up only when I least expected it. But if something terrible waited, at least Ruth would be three thousand miles away.

The despair of letting her go had by this time sunk even deeper in my gut. But you could grow used to these things. People lost limbs, beliefs, loved ones . . . They went on. I'd seen gratuitous invasions and barbarism, mass executions, piracy, rape, grievous tyranny, torture, enslavement, gruesome epidemics. People went on. And I did too, going through the motions of day-to-day life with a hole in my heart, stepping stone to stone without looking into the distance. I'd learned long ago to welcome life's small pleasures with or without company, and I expected that time—my version of time—would heal even this wound eventually. Ruth had brought me delight, yes, but delight, by its very nature, is temporary. If it endured, it wouldn't feel like delight anymore. Yet this time the misery felt particularly pointless, like waiting for a wound to heal, open up again, heal, and reopen in an endless cycle without meaning or purpose. Pleasure ought to be more than just relief from pain.

I remembered the smell of her hair, the texture fine as a baby chick's. Her beauty was deeper than time, but there was no real vanity to her. Why did I have to be an instrument of her pain?

Months went by, then a year. No sign of The Beast. I dreamed of Ruth. Always in danger. Sometimes she was callous, her face like stone that I'd carved into being with my own selfishness. The Beast laughed unseen as though he'd created the dreams to haunt me.

Evelyn became a regular at Pamela's place. Ruth must have told her about it. A good jazz place is hard to find. Evelyn, who'd played clarinet in a university marching band, knew just enough about what the musicians were doing to get them eating out of her bony hand. She became a surrogate grumpy aunt or sister they wanted to please. Sometimes she'd show up with a date, but you rarely saw the same man twice. We established a truce without acknowledging there'd been a war and never discussed Ruth, even after she crashed the cover of *The New York Times Book Review* with her *Mary Shelley: Frankenstein's First Victim*. Ruth Canby very quickly became a crossover intellectual in demand, along the lines of the late William F. Buckley, except this model was a bewitching, progressive female who lacked Buckley's grudges, tics, and sinister subterfuge. Arbiters of what was important were enthralled by her quick mind and unpretentious glamour. Paparazzi competed to capture her beguiling essence. *Der Spiegel* jumped in front of the pack with a cover that became an instant Pop Art poster—a head-to-toe, smiling, slender, breathless Ruth pulling off her bathing cap while emerging from a pool at Columbia. I didn't know whether swimming laps was a new or accustomed activity. By rushing through our relationship, not allowing it to evolve naturally, I'd been cheated out of making such discoveries on my own, and had to watch through a media filter along with everyone else. One sleepless night I caught her on both MTV and Charlie Rose. *The Economist* called Ruth Canby "an acknowledged leader of the new, no-nonsense, open-minded breed of American thinker" whose pinpoint prose "shot beams of penetrating light into hungry minds, as well as plenty of minds that hadn't been aware they were hungry before she made them aware of it."

Her book painted Mary Shelley as an oracle who foresaw that the industrial and technological revolutions would harness unforeseen consequences such as climate change, frequent, deadlier brushfire wars, and affluent consumers who hatched their offspring by choosing spores off DNA menus. As petro-poisons and credit default swaps raced ahead at electro-digital speed, humankind, she wrote, mimicked Victor Frankenstein in neglecting to master their effects or even to contemplate them before they were released upon the world. But now, she said, there were powerful new mass media to carpet-bomb its consumers with amoral vulgarity, up-ending ethics and taste at near-light speed. Not even Shelley, observed Ruth, had foreseen that Frankenstein's creature would become the world's electronic babysitter, transfixing and shaping minds from infancy. She revived a trenchant statement by F. Scott Fitzgerald: "The victor belongs to the spoils."

Ruth's success surprised me less than you might imagine. I'd already seen two hundred generations. I understood how special she was. From the furthest reaches of the balcony she'd unlocked more mysteries than I'd managed from my orchestra seat. Most of what's considered history is a shaggy dog story about a tiny slice of humankind—the rulers. That fact is widely known but rarely acted upon. Ruth however, threaded it into the fiber of her analysis.

Stalking her on the Net, I came across a photo of her at Lincoln Center with Michel Houellebecq, a writer who'd stormed the French literary scene with a series of novels that told uncomfortable truths about the relationship between sex and money in the modern world. Googling him, I learned that his hippie mother had abandoned him at birth to rela-tives. After he achieved success she wrote a book calling him a stupid little bastard. I followed the romance with diligence and pain and was delighted to see it end.

With Ruth's voice and face popping out at me from around every corner, how could I even begin to forget her? Not since Tamara had I so despised my peculiar condition—a condition that now felt like centuries of loss and disappointment.

CHAPTER 11

RUTH

Preparing to move across the country as the Lenny clock ticked away felt like being forced to hum a little tune while falling off a roof. As I stared at my belongings, I decided to leave behind all the useless shards of the past that followed me around for no good reason. I kept some clothes and books and abandoned the rest. When you've had no family, your mementoes are impersonal merchandise masquerading as something they could never be, and I was weary of the charade.

I grew up listening wistfully to tales of kids adopted by their foster parents. Eventually I decided these were fairy tales for orphans, or, more likely, that no one chose me because I was a defective model. But I also couldn't help noticing that the families I stayed with were always in serious distress and had been long before I arrived. Arranging to get me was a financial decision, a desperate attempt to get some of the bills paid and had little to do with me personally.

By the time I was eleven or twelve I'd learned to keep my foster heart hidden behind razor wire, though I opened it a little to an agency-appointed mom named Alice. She was a part-time supermarket cashier who had three kids of her own, two black hairs on her chin, and every once in a while felt like what I imagined a mother to be. Alice taught me how to sew and bought me presents like a totally uncool backpack that was a goldmine for nasty kids looking for someone to torment.

After saving all her coins for two years, Alice finally bought something for herself—a brand new refrigerator. But the door somehow got scratched the very first week, and the small gouge in the metal I could barely see represented to her all the reasons her life never went the way it was supposed to. My presence in her home was more proof of her lousy luck. Deciding I'd perpetrated the scratch, she beat the hell out of me with such red-eyed mania that we couldn't hide the marks and the school reported her. My cover story kept Alice out of jail, but her career as a foster parent was finished.

My job was to grow up in an Ozzie and Harriet family of never-faltering sweetness and caring, everyone white, suburban, clean, and calm, where any anguish would prove to be short-lived, unjustified, and worthy of one or two small jokes. But I'd failed miserably and shouldered the responsibility like Frankenstein's creature, who tried to blame his creator yet mostly despised himself for the radically non-conforming circumstances of his background.

You like to know what things mean, particularly the pivotal events in your own life. But my origins were a tenacious mystery spawning enigmas, stories that had no explanation or even a real ending. I felt I was in one of those art films that will eventually just stop somewhere in what seems like the middle. Lenny was only the latest mystery.

With my belongings pretty much disposed of, I had too much time to envision our goodbye. A scene of farewell offered the false hope that he'd change his mind and would lead only to additional suffering. So I skipped it. I told him I'd be leaving Thursday and flew out Wednesday. I was pretty sure he'd understand. But I mourned the hours we lost because of my cowardice.

Exiting a taxi at dawn, I delivered myself to airport functionaries who barked instructions as I crept forward with other travel inmates trying to get out of L.A. *Photo and travel documents out, shoes and belts off, luggage there, not here. Do we detect a water bottle? Laptops out of their cases, dummies, can't*

you understand antagonism? Halt, sit, scramble, halt, proceed.
No, we don't want to see your damn photo I.D. again.

Ninety minutes later we squeezed into the plane, stashed our pitiful whatnots in our tin sanctum, and settled in to breathe deeply each other's microbes. *Eleven jets ahead of us, yes, we have no food, we'll serve this instead. Below are the Tetons. Tray tables down, careful, tossed luggage splits skulls, don't forget any of your crap, and thanks for flying with us, assholes. Connecting to another flight here at JFK? Lucky you.*

We passed through a maze of sterile, fetid alcoves into a Stalinist meat locker, and finally found what most of us agreed was our designated luggage carousel. No, wrong one. Ours must be the one over there that just started belching noise. We crossed fingers as our carefully compiled belongings bumped, thudded, circled. *Screw the others, just don't lose mine.* Ooh, got it! Tore my way toward, please God, an exit.

In his sequel to *Catch-22*, Joseph Heller theorized that hell—not figurative hell but true hell—was New York's Port Authority Bus Terminal. He was off by a few miles only, because he didn't live long enough to come through JFK during the post-Nine-Eleven terror.

I stumbled through the glass doors ragged, stinking, bereaved, on the frazzled edge of a fetal position. "How was your flight?" This from brisk Task Force administrator Sally, a Nigerian who'd read philosophy at Cambridge and was miffed I hadn't flown first class. "A miscommunication," she said with just a pinch of accusation in her tone. Sally and a uniformed driver guided me into a Mercedes and powered me across the river to a fabulous furnished co-op at Seventy-Ninth and Amsterdam. Tennis court on the roof, twenty-four hour security, etc. The apartment belonged to a Task Force professor who'd be gone at least a year, maybe two. My employer was subsidizing both ends of our lease, making my monthly cost lower than the co-op fee. Included was a twice-a-week visit from what turned out to be a bacteria-phobic cleaning woman from Slovenia.

The rooms had a razor-like smoothness to them, everything black, white, or chrome. Critics might find it stark or artificial. I adored it. Down below, the streets crackled with an urban vitality that's as addicting as any chemical. Within seventy-two hours I'd be a smug New York zealot who couldn't imagine how I'd ever managed to live elsewhere. Strolling through the irresistible turmoil I recalled how adults crossing a street in L.A. affected a peculiar, twisted smile, as if to say they were embarrassed to be outside their car, but it was just a temporary condition and soon they'd be back where they belong.

◈

When I reported to the Task Force suite at Rockefeller Center, the receptionist placed me in the custody of Jorge, who smelled like orchids and looked like a thirtyish Ricardo Montalbán. His crisp, pinstriped suit, whiter-than-white pocket handkerchief, and gleaming footwear had been planned better than both Iraq invasions. After performing a little half-bow he led me across a polished stone floor toward some destination whose name I didn't catch. We passed through lengthy corridors dimly lit by occasional lamps imbedded in the walls, giving passageways the look and feel of well-scrubbed catacombs. Cool, mysterious breezes swept subtly past us. I stamped the obligatory first-day smile on my face as smartly attired employees walking in the other direction pretended to have no interest in me. I was tempted to turn around and wave as they stared at my back. They were dressed so meticulously that my carefully chosen new-employee outfit rated no more than a B-minus here. Except for expansive Jorge, everyone spoke in muted tones, creating an almost continuous hallway murmur.

My (private) office made my recent setup in California look like the back of a radiator shop. For a moment I thought Jorge was kidding when he explained I was free to order all new furniture if I didn't like this stuff. On my desk was a neat stack of papers awaiting my signature that included a book contract from a prestigious publisher paying me a hundred-fifty-thousand dollar advance. Though it wasn't John Grisham money, it was, I'd been assured, astronomical for a book of its type.

Jorge defined his own position as "associate administrator" and a couple of times referred to me as one of the "resident scholars." "You share me with Dr. Braslow," he said, "but he prefers to work from home in Southampton and rarely even calls, so in truth I belong to you," whereupon he opened his eyes a bit wider, implying a vaster panorama of services than I cared to know about. But his other features remained fixed, so in that sense he said it with a straight face. Jorge could no doubt sell Ferraris or sex toys with that same straight face. I would find out later that he was a predatory bisexual who'd slept with half the night-clubbers in the Dominican Republic and was now blazing a second trail through New York.

As I tried out my desk, Jorge sat down without being asked, leaned in close to explain the phone system, told me when to expect my first paycheck, and apologized profusely for Borges, whose connection from Morocco had been waylaid by a disobedient sandstorm. "The dean will greet you personally tomorrow, I'm sure. But in the meantime, don't be afraid to ask me anything, Dr. Canby. I do fabulous phone, manipulate bureaucracies, Google up the impossible. I find art objects. I know where to get the best corned beef on rye in the city." Then he raised his eyebrows, rose, placed his orchid butt on the edge of my desk and slid close again as he spoke tenderly of the spectacular sushi right down the street. I looked up at him impassively from my state-of-the-art, ergonomic chair. A barely perceptible suggestion of a leer crossed his close-shaved face as he made two or three escalating remarks that, it became clear, were what he presumed to be witty references to raw fish and cunt. This experience was like engaging in what appears to be normal conversation with someone in a darkened room whom you finally identify as the severed head of a dog. Meanwhile, apparently encouraged by my silence, Jorge asked me to dinner. Emerging from shock, I asked him, "You said you find things, right?"

He nodded.

"Good. Get your ass off my desk and go find yourself a cardboard box. You're fired. Who does administrative personnel around here?"

He snapped to a standing position like my desk was a hot stove and uttered a name through the cracks of his fallen face. I dialed zero and asked for a Lacy Steinberg. "This is Ruth Canby," I told her. "Mr.— Excuse me." I looked up. "What's your last name?"

"You're not really on the faculty," Jorge sputtered. "You're no better than me."

"Give me a moment," I told Steinberg. I lowered the phone and looked up at Jorge. "I never said I was better than you. What I said is you're fired. I will not work with you. Go."

Jorge drew near again. He appeared on the cusp of assault or flight, as though little red demons shouted conflicting advice, one in each ear. I brought the phone close enough for Steinberg to hear. "Get out or I'll call the cops."

In half an hour Sally was back, this time as my assistant. She made no mention of Jorge.

"I wondered how long it would take you to dismiss Jorge," Borges told me in his office the next day. "You beat the old record by a mile."

He was once again dressed like a cross between a hipster pirate of Penzance and a gypsy lunatic—South Pacific jewelry, old jeans and faded green t-shirt with a tear along a shoulder allowing a generous peek at his sinewy biceps. A maroon bandana circled his dark yellow hippie hair. With all his "associate administrators" dressed for tea at Windsor Palace, his freakish clothing paraded Borges's power like no Versace leather or Patek Phillipe could, placing him not just above his staffers, but beyond them. I recall Evelyn telling me of Hollywood barons who showed their dominance by dressing beneath rather than above their subordinates.

"Evidently you get a kick out of hazing rookies," I told him.

"I had to assign Jorge. Internal politics. He's a madman, but he's a harmless madman. Occasionally the exigencies of fund-raising force me to hire somebody's oddball nephew. It's not something I like to do, and I try not to let any of it touch our scholars. Sometimes I just can't avoid it. I do apologize. But allow me to point out that in the last five years three Columbia professors have won Nobels. Two were from this Task Force. Not bad for a faculty that couldn't fill a club car. It takes money to do that. Lots of it. Jorge was no joke, Dr. Canby, but neither is the handsome salary, the book contract, the apartment, or any of the other perks you have yet to discover. We select our scholars more carefully than you imagine. If it weren't for all the so-called think tanks out there I'd welcome our being called a think tank because that's what you're paid to do here—think. And that's all you have to do, other than publish those thoughts from time to time. I know you'll do great things, and I'll be particularly gratified because I plucked you out of a shit-hole. As for Jorge, I'm pleased you reacted so forcefully. But I'm curious. Weren't you just a bit frightened of the result? What if we'd believed his story instead of yours?"

"I told you once I'm not afraid of you."

Sally had been assigned to me only temporarily and was soon replaced by Sparky, an expectant mother from Kentucky on parole for peddling crystal meth. She was also fluent in Chinese and Arabic. Many of the people I met around the Task Force possessed traits, habits, and accomplishments in odd combinations. Every time you turned a corner you ran into a one-legged pole-vaulter or something. They had interesting histories, but they didn't have anything interesting to say, at least not to me.

What I didn't run into were other scholars. Recruits worked out of the office only a short while and then made other arrangements. Except for Borges, everyone I met was an "associate administrator," and there seemed to be an excessive number of these grandiosely titled clerks. They apparently spent an hour or more getting dressed each morning, and the rest of the day purring to each other in snide, conspiratorial tones. On more than one occasion the murmuring stopped dead as I entered a room.

Jorge was still on staff but kept a wide berth. As he'd pointed out, I wasn't quite faculty. It placed me in a limbo that disturbed the order of things. The clerks harbored a crazy grudge against me, as though I were a bounder who'd intruded into their world from across the Great Wall. Everyone was polite, no one was friendly. I lunched alone.

Borges behaved himself, but I made a private rule not to meet him anywhere outside the office. I broke the rule my second week when he introduced me to my editor at the publishing house, a Mr. Terrance Saldo, over lunch at a brilliant little French bistro. Saldo was a smallish neurotic and a serial name-dropper who kept his nose so far up Borges's ass I don't know how either of them managed to eat. In a replay of our one phone call, Saldo barely inquired about my book's subject matter. Now he promised to rush me into print within six months of my manuscript's completion.

"That's lovely, Terrance," Borges told him. "But don't heave it over the side like table scraps. Weave your marketing magic."

"Fear not," Saldo pledged. "Plan A is the plan."

It was no secret that a vast majority of manuscripts perished like fruit flies, barely scanned by besieged agents and publishing houses. Yet the tiny sliver that made it into print amounted to thousands of books a year. Almost all expired within a few weeks. Bookstore chains showed remarkably little patience for titles that didn't fly off the shelves. While the fix was in for big books with big backing from big publishers, sales for the vast majority of titles were left to the vagaries of dying independent bookstores and the Internet.

I was uncertain whether Saldo or anyone else could get anyone to care about a book that focused on Mary Shelley, but clearly I was receiving special treatment, which made me uncomfortable even after Evelyn's repeated telephonic and emailed reminders that as long as I worked diligently, there was no shame in making use of my new connections: "Why not let the good guys in on it for a change?"

Before you start, writing a book looks impossible, like trying to build a submarine all by yourself. But after you begin welding things into place it starts to feel more achievable. In my case I already knew plenty about Shelley, I knew what I wanted to say about her and her relevance to our time. I had all my notes ready. Now all I had to do was organize them and build my book, ruthlessly throwing out everything that wasn't engaging.

Trouble was, the spooky, off-center feel of the office made it difficult for me to work there comfortably. I tried writing at home, but that was even worse. With my whole life going on under one ceiling, my designer retreat started to feel like a jail cell. So mornings I joined the yuppie laptop legion on the coffee shop circuit, trying different neighborhood cafes until I found the right chemical mix of coffee and ambience. Watching other customers hunched over their machines, I'd try to guess what they were working on: Screenplays? Sales campaigns? Hydrogen power? The woman with the iced tea and the green jeans could be the next Norman Mailer or a dilettante. I knew there were plenty of creative people around, but I didn't know how to meet them. I'd see many of the same customers day after day. Though we barely spoke, we had a bond—a need for human contact, even if it meant having to listen to each other's phone business while we pursued our solitary tasks. Once or twice a week I switched gears and took the A train to campus, where I worked out of the law library and swam laps in the pool (the Task Force had set me up with a faculty card despite my limbo status).

In L.A. I'd been suspended in a gray dimension where anything hopeful would always prove a delusion. Now, with a publisher and a prestigious think tank betting on me, I didn't feel quite so crazy betting on myself.

How often did I think of Lenny? Perhaps always. Minds race into nooks and crannies day and night, conscious or not. Imagining myself in his arms again was an unbearably exquisite poison.

> *As Earth lies bare to heaven above!*
> *How is it under our control*
> *To love or not to love?*

Robert Browning understood, but he wasn't around to give me a hug.

I can't say with certainty what it's like for ordinary people who find love, because the world reminds me every day that I'm peculiar, an orphan. Possibly I feel love differently. But at times it was comforting to remember that somewhere in the world a companion soul existed, a person who adored me, cherished me. I knew it for sure. This was no case of unrequited love. It was mystery beating me with a hammer.

Of course it was absurd to be faithful to a man who'd sent me away with such finality. And after awhile I was coaxed onto a party circuit. Although my precise station within the think tank remained unclear, out in the city I was a Task Force scholar, which gave me a fairly thick slice of status.

"This won't be a boy-girl date," Borges assured me. "I just want to introduce you to some interesting people." And he pulled me aboard a merry-go-round of cocktail and dinner parties that must have begun circling the calendar decades earlier and now fed off its own energy. Writers, performers, impresarios, politicians, publicists, fashionistas, and always of course, the idle rich, who, despite a murderous economy, remained rich as ever, their impregnable assets tinkling like platinum bells.

Every once in a while Borges would try to reconfigure the nature of our relationship back to that California night.

"Look, Borges, this is getting irritating."

"Call a cop then. But give me a jury of twelve heterosexual men. One look at you and they'll understand."

"No one's calling the cops, Borges. I owe you. When's your birthday? I'll buy you a real shirt and we'll be even."

"You owe me nothing. But it would be nice if you'd stop insulting my— What should we call it? Fashion sense, for lack of a better term. Ooh, you laughed at me, didn't you?"

"Did not."

"You kept it inside, but I felt the lash. Look, Ruth, if the memory of that night is half as strong for you as it is for me, this is crazy. I'd crawl to Brooklyn for another night like that."

"Cut it out."

"All you have to do is smile and nod your head."

I brushed him off a hundred different ways, but he had a point. It *was* at least slightly ridiculous for two adults to pretend not to remember something they both remembered well. Propositions came from others too, and both genders. On two occasions from teams on the lookout for new threesomes and foursomes. I routinely turned everyone down and sometimes wondered why.

CHAPTER 12

LENNY

This feels more like a memory than a dream. Trying to distinguish details is like digging through a mountain of bones. I think of it as a horse, but it may have been an ox. I remember only its eyes bulging in torment as the scourging continued to body, head, and yes, even those tortured eyes. The wagon driver cursed in a language I don't recall, taking breaks before considering where to strike next. A dusty traveler stepped out of the crowd and spoke to him. The driver raised his whip threateningly and in one lightning move the traveler pulled a blade from his tunic and thrust it through the man's eye deep into his skull. I was close enough to hear a ripping sound. The lifeless body crumpled to the ground. The traveler placed a foot across the dead teeth and yanked his weapon from the skull. He knelt over the dying animal, spoke softly into its ear, and plunged his blade between its eyes. There was a grunt, a whoosh of air, then silence. Retrieving the blade again, the stranger wiped the blood across the dead man's chest. The traveler looked straight into my soul. I fled.

At first I recalled the stranger as a friend to the beast. Ultimately in my mind he became simply The Beast.

❖

It was almost time to fashion a new identity and move on. I thought I'd try Montreal next. It had nothing to do with The Beast. If a confrontation were at hand, he'd find me in Canada as easily as Los Angeles.

One night at Pamela's, Evelyn, after too many whiskey sours, broke our rule and spoke of Ruth, describing to Pamela the regiment of suitors pursuing her beautiful, famous New York friend that included some prominent intellect on everybody's invitation list who was "tall, handsome," blah, blah, blah. She made sure I was in earshot. A part of me was desperate for such intelligence all the while, and now that I was hearing it I couldn't bear it. I thought harder about Montreal as I steered Jubal toward the other end of the bar. No band that night. It was the usual jazz club pattern. They opened with big plans and high ideals, but the jazz population is aging and shrinking, and live entertainment slips from five or six nights a week down to one or two. Next thing you knew a new owner turns the place into a sushi joint.

And I didn't have Ruth anymore.

"'Stead of walking around miserable," Jubal said, "why don't you go claim what's yours?"

"She's a best-selling celebrity and I'm a half-assed rent-a-cop living in somebody else's house," I said, hanging on to my story that it was Ruth who'd severed the relationship. The necessity of adding more lies to support the original lie made escape to Montreal seem even more attractive.

"She gave a damn about any of that, Evelyn wouldn't talk that way."

Evelyn, apparently not finished with me, carried her glass our way, a taut, joyless smile on her lips. Crap. But she had another target in mind. "I don't suppose you remember me," she said to a man on the next stool. He and the woman with him, probably his wife, looked like members of a low-grade country club.

He held a finger up and nodded, as though grabbing a memory from the air. "Eleanor, isn't it?" he said. "Nice to see you." He turned to his companion. "Betty, this is Eleanor."

Evelyn didn't correct him. "Hey, remember the other night? You asked the band to do these songs? What the fuck songs were they again?"

"I don't recall," he said, still pretending the conversation was friendly.

"Sure you do. C'mon, what was it? Something from— I know. *Cats*. It was, wasn't it?"

"It . . . might have been from *Mama Mia!*"

Evelyn looked at him like he'd just taken a dump on the bar. The look was not only intense, but sustained. Each time he thought it must be finished he raised his eyes to find Evelyn still glaring at him. Finally he drained his wine glass and stepped away from his stool. "Sorry, we gotta go." He addressed his companion. "Betty?"

"I'm done," Betty squealed. They moved out as though escaping flames.

"Well listen," Evelyn shouted after them, "the musicians, they just love doing *South Pacific, Cats,* all a that stuff. So come back another time. When they're here. Okay?" She wasn't slurring her words, teetering, or any of that, but she must have been pretty plastered.

Pamela, sitting at the bar with a cup of coffee and a stack of invoices, advised Evelyn, "Next time you chase somebody out, you might want to leave a little skin on their bones." But she didn't seem terribly bothered.

"Sorry. I'll leave a big tip."

"You always leave a big tip," Jubal told her. "That don't impress us no more. Besides, Miles did 'Surrey with the Fringe on Top' from *Oklahoma*. Miles ain't cool enough for you?"

"That jerk, he tried to pick me up," Evelyn explained. "And tonight he comes in with a wife and a wedding ring."

"Screw 'em then, honey," Pamela said. "We don't need creeps like that hanging around."

"Thanks. I like you."

"I like you too."

"No, really, I like you a lot."

Pamela leaned across the bar and hugged Evelyn, who was momentarily on the edge of tears, but it passed.

"That guy has to be one of the ten most boring people in America," said Evelyn, who now looked less melancholy and perhaps even amused. "You know what he talked about? Setting up his new real estate office. Wow, talk about seductive material. On and on . . . told me about the windows that didn't fit right at first, the drywall contractor, the super-smart young guy he brought in to handle residential properties so he could concentrate on commercial properties. I don't think I asked him one question through any of it."

"And you just let him?" Pamela asked her.

"I don't know, I was in this mode where I decided I need to be more patient with people, so it was like the perfect storm. This guy, anyone who doesn't tell him to fuck off, he figures they're fascinated."

"If we keep out all the bores and snakes," Pamela said, "how we supposed to pay the rent?"

"I resent that," Jubal said.

Evelyn: "He probably prowls the city looking for people who'll let him babble on like that. I wanted to— Ah, to hell with him." She turned to me. "It's my birthday, Lenny."

I congratulated her as she drained her glass, drunk and possibly anorexic in a dying saloon.

"I thank you. You don't ask me how old I am. You know why not?"

"I don't—"

"'Cause I'm old. If I were young you'd ask."

"But—"

"That's okay, you were just being polite. This is one of those blockbuster birthdays—a decade marker, know what I mean? You'll see. It goes fast. But I guess everyone says that. It's hard to say or do anything original about getting old. How old're you, Lenny?"

"You need a ride home?" I asked her.

"He won't tell anybody. Mysterious. Can I see your driver's license?"

I shook my head.

"Would it tell me the truth?" She waited. "He doesn't say. But he doesn't lie either. Yeah, Lenny's mysterious. He can be nice, but he wasn't so nice to Ruth, were you Lenny?"

"Look, Evelyn—"

"My little brother's a junky."

"I'm sorry."

"We put him in this detox program up in the Valley? They had family night once a week. Families of the patients or addicts or drunks or whatever they were. The preferred term seemed to be users. It's a good word. They use up everything and everyone around them. Anyway, the families were supposed to sit in group and go, you know, there, there. There, there. It was the first time Joey had been in a program so I was dumb enough to show up. Everyone sits in a circle bitching about being lied to and stolen from and getting their hearts broken a thousand ways by their user losers. There was this young Goth woman—you know, all in black, black lipstick, everything. She's bitching more than anyone. Her boyfriend's a hard-core crystal meth addict. A tweaker. He was dealing too, probably. And the guy leading the group was giving Goth Girl all sorts of sympathy. On and on it goes. How awful it must be for her. There, there. I realized I'd seen the boyfriend when I visited Joey. Also in a black costume. Bleached-out face, tattoos on his neck. Finally I asked her, 'How long have you been with him?' She thinks awhile, then answers maybe five weeks. Which means it was probably less.

" 'Did you know he was shooting crystal meth,' " I ask her, 'when you first got involved with him?' She hems and haws but finally admits she found out pretty early.

" 'You move in with a rattlesnake,' I tell her, 'he bites you, and we're all supposed to be surprised?' We don't scold people here for choices they made in the past, the group leader says, except he said it in some kind of psychobabble. It's unhealthy, he says. He's a little, washed-out redheaded guy, a serious drunk, I find out later.

"The girlfriend explains her boyfriend has so many wonderful qualities though, like he's another Gandhi or something. 'Look,' I said, 'the rest of us are here because we're family. We didn't *choose* people with substance abuse problems. They *became* people with substance abuse problems.' I mean, I drove all the way to Van Nuys to hear this?"

"You know," Jubal says, "some of these—"

"Here's the point," Evelyn interrupted him. She looked at me. "Ruth's not Goth Girl looking to get bruised. She didn't deserve your crap."

"Give the man a break," Jubal said.

Evelyn: "She had such a rotten childhood, you know? But she overcame that and she's so sweet and . . . you come along and— You were so fucking cruel. You're a moron. You know that?"

"Happy birthday," I said, leaving some bills on the nearly deserted bar.

She shouted after me. "She's got Anton Borges now, buster! She doesn't need *you* anymore."

Anton Borges. Well I hoped Anton Borges, whoever he was, would make her happy. The name helped me picture him in my mind. He looked like Desi Arnaz. Good-looking fellow, Desi Arnaz. The bastard.

RUTH

I was on a no-frills book tour at a Walmart in Columbus, Ohio, seated next to the radishes. Each minute I spent there took a month. Customers avoided eye contact with pitiful me as I smiled and tried to project it was okay that no one wanted to even speak to me, much less ask me to sign a book. I tried to hide my pile of unsold copies under my little table so I wouldn't look quite so pathetic. Finally, a woman with a whimpering toddler in her pushcart approached and asked me where the hardware section was. You can bet that never happened to Bob Woodward. That's when Saldo called from the publisher's office.

"You're not going to believe this." He was giggling like a ten-year-old.

"What?" I said.

He wanted me to guess.

"No, just tell me. I need to help someone locate a Phillips screwdriver."

His impeccable source at the *Times*, he said, leaked word that it was planning a huge splash on my book, a front-page rave review that said I'd used Shelley as a starting point to redirect "the conversation," whatever that was, down a livelier and potentially more fortuitous path. That same day the publisher flew out a publicist to hold my hand, and I started life under the big top. Later I found out that plenty of titles receiving similar pushes from the *Times* died quick deaths anyway. But this time the rest of the media jumped on the train, and just like that I was a best-selling author. Here's the irony though. The vulgarization of Shelley's Frankenstein was repeating itself. The monster was all the rage, but I'd become an unwilling agent of yet another wave of misinterpretation and sensationalist exploitation. The Hollywood shredder all over again.

Also, the interviewers, for the most part, weren't terribly interested in discussing Shelley or my book because they hadn't read either of us. They mostly wanted to focus on my personal life. Drama, confession, tears, fornication, incest, anything along those lines. So I told them my parents were former members of the Baader-Meinhof gang who'd quit violent rebellion in Germany to build new lives in Alaska. I borrowed the idea from Bob Dylan, who discovered decades earlier that interviews are a lot more fun if you make up all the answers. Any data about me that predated my college years, I said, had been hacked into by my cunning fugitive parents, whom I hadn't heard from in years and whose real names I'd never learned. I didn't say this to bump up sales, though that's what it did. The publicist kept extending my tour—signings, interviews, airports, hotels, tedium. Finally I just booked a flight back to New York.

You can't do that, the publicist said. You have to strike while the iron's hot. But all I wanted to do was take a break from media madness and begin my next book. She looked at me like I was dating O.J.

"All right, then," she said. She's talking, she figures, to a psycho and she'd better not excite me. "Do . . ." she whizzed around on her Blackberry, ". . . just four more before you go back. Then rest . . ." more fumbling with her little gizmo, ". . . three days before you go out again."

But she'd have to find someone else to fill Elvis' shoes. "And another thing," I told her. "If I ever hit the circuit again I won't deal with interviewers who haven't read the book. At the signings I get good questions from readers, but interviewers all want to know my sign and who I'm dating."

"If you make preconditions they'll eat you alive," she said.

"Tell that to Pynchon," I said.

"Who's Pynchon?" asked the publicity lady.

"Somebody who calls his own shots," I said.

That, she said, must be why she never heard of him.

An hour after I got home I went to work. Words and ideas flowed and I wanted to capture them before they got away. Fortunately my semi-fame didn't change much of anything back at the old coffee shop. New Yorkers are good about that. One day a little man tripped over my laptop cord. His plastic bottle of vitamin water flew straight into a philodendron.

"I'm so terribly sorry," I said.

"No you're not. You're one of *them*, aren't you?"

Oh my God.

"Gotcha," he said, letting out a nice healthy laugh.

This began my friendship with Ben.

CHAPTER 13

LENNY

Centuries ago, riding north of the Black Forest, I spotted a dead wolf nailed trophy-like to a shed at the edge of the road. He hung there like an old coat. Some peasant must have struggled to get all that dead weight up there, making me wonder whether he'd held a personal grudge against the animal. The face, debased and shrunken, was folded into furry wrinkles of despair and suffering, as though in its last moment the wolf understood the fullness and finality of its own death. The jowly, permanently disgruntled face of Trianon the hedge fund manager reminded me of that wolf. But instead of stalking peasant flocks he obsessively watched stock quotes moving across the bottom of his TV screen. He also loved to talk back to the screen images of politicians as they made their pronouncements to the cameras. "Think about the children," he'd say in a derisive, burlesque tone, mocking the idea and those who profess it while implying that anyone who claims to care about the needy always hides selfish motives.

Trianon breathed and spoke in grunts and half-grunts, exhaling an inexhaustible gravel of restless indifference. You prayed for him to clear his throat. When he ate, it was like listening to a machine chew up tree parts. He was clearly impressed by the delinquent aura that surrounded Powell, while ex-con Powell longed to be accepted by rich white people and mostly had to settle for dwarfed personalities like Trianon. They were a symbiotic pair, but I couldn't tell whether Powell was the water buffalo that attracted parasites or the tickbird that ate them off Trianon's ass.

Trianon, a lap-dance addict, apparently was well known on the nude bar circuit, where it was rumored he left a long, twisted trail of hundred dollar bills and jizzum stains. It was the subject of ongoing banter between him and Powell, who, doggedly faithful to his wife, refused to accompany him to his strip dives and late-night clubs. As a compromise, Trianon would invite Powell to his Coliseum-sized compound on Mulholland, where he ordered out for whores, disc jockeys, Thanksgiving turkeys, whatever he felt like. On this particular evening he'd rented two blondes in little black dresses from a strip joint near the airport. I wasn't sure whether they were the same ones from the Blankenship funeral.

Powell was envious that Trianon could pull his stock market scams high above the weather, while he had to operate down in the part of the economy where rats scramble for garbage. Just now he was inquiring what it cost Trianon to get a specific paragraph attached to a congressional tax bill.

"We don't put it in those terms, Ray," replied Trianon, sifting his words through his customary throat gravel. He sat sandwiched between the two blondes on a white, L-shaped sofa the size of a gondola, caressing with short, nervous fingers one cute, panty-hosed knee in each hand, probably more to stake out ownership than to reap a sensual dividend. The blondes were in their early twenties, if that. He occasionally let go of a knee to sip a bright green drink on the coffee table that looked misleadingly cheerful. Some kind of French concoction.

"We contribute to public servants to gain access, the same as you," Trianon said, "but we don't write the laws. That's what I'd tell the media anyway, if they asked me. But you know what? They never do. They just want to know what I'm buying or selling. Excuse me. I need to hear this." He turned the sound up on the financial channel. I'd have thought he had more exclusive sources of information. Maybe he just wanted to know what the suckers were being told. After taking a couple of quick calls, he slipped into a snooze born of the green concoction and possibly other substances. I was fairly certain he hadn't screwed either of his blondes, and now I wondered whether he'd ever get around to it.

Powell had too much dignity to sit there and take it while his host caught a nap, but before he could leave he took a call on his cell. "This might take a while," he told me, moving toward another room for privacy. That left me sitting with a comically snoring Trianon and the two blondes. One searched for the remote. The other rose from the sofa, walked directly across the Persian carpet, and planted herself in front of me, her slender waist only a few provocative inches from my nose. With one white boot set forward as though she were posing on a runway, she bent down and whispered, "Got a cigarette?" Depraved male that I am, I tilted my head to signal that we should conduct this business down the hall. I doubt I'd heard ten words out of this young woman or her partner in two hours, and I was intrigued. Maybe she was one of those brilliant hooker-scholars of urban myth or a sex slave seeking rescue. She shot me a puzzled glance, but carrying a tiny, spangled purse, she followed me as I left the room. I headed down a hallway and opened a door that led into one of the many bedrooms. She followed me inside, closed it, and looked at me expectantly.

"Sorry, I don't smoke." I tried to say it as innocently and naturally as I could. Look, I know she was approximately 3,978 years my junior. But it's hard to find women my own age.

"Nervy bastard, aren't you?"

"Just captivated." I looked down at the king-sized bed. "Okay if I sit down?"

"You're a *double* nervy bastard." She dived onto the bed with a giggle. Lying on her stomach, she bent her knees and raised her ankles in the air as she lazily rested her chin on her baby-smooth fist and looked up at me with big, brown eyes. "What're you doing with these creeps?"

"I could ask you the same question," I said, seating myself next to her. I tried to do it as lightly and unobtrusively as possible.

"I know where he keeps the coke." She brought her mouth close and I kissed her. She had natural curls and a pixie-ish face, but her eyes were the traditionally hard and calculating eyes of whoredom.

"So you're just using me." I lightly traced my fingers across the back of her head. Alas, hairspray.

"We can share."

"What's your name?"

"Tony, with a 'Y.' Everybody wants to spell it with an 'I' cause I'm a girl."

"The bastards."

"You're funny, aren't you?"

"If you say so." I kissed her again.

"That was better."

"I thought so too," I said, my lips still close to hers.

"Where you from?"

"Israel, originally."

"You must have come over when you were a little kid. I used to go out with a guy, he was from— Where was it? Syria. He sure didn't like you guys."

"Israelis? Or Jews?"

"Both." She barely touched her lips to mine, breathing into me.

I nuzzled her ear. "You're sexy when you talk politics."

I try to reconcile the world's seething, seemingly genetic loathing for Jews with its insistence that moral and religious structures be based on Jewish mythology. Not long ago, after centuries of absence, I returned to the land of my birth where I ascertained again that Israeli character ranged from bastardly to saintly pretty much like everywhere else. Like the ancient Hebrews as well. So why are Jews depicted as a stubborn cult of black magic demons? Sinister, eerily capable beings that perennially intrude into the lives of honest folk. Even creative geniuses like Shakespeare, Dostoyevsky, and F. Scott Fitzgerald thought so. I had a professor in Belgium who contended the foundation for these beliefs was the Gospel of John, which, unlike the other three, blamed neither Pharisees nor priests for Jesus's death, but generic "Jews." "John himself was a Jew," the professor said. "So he must have known what he was talking about, don't you think?" A typical European comment. And off the mark. The seeds of anti-Semitism were planted much earlier. Before my father ascended Mount Moriah, we were like everyone else. When the two of us returned to the plain we were a people apart, bound by a covenant.

And two thousand years later the Lord himself played the role of Abraham. This time the son received no last-minute reprieve. More blood, more hocus-pocus. By that time I'd long since moved on to other lands. After Emperor Titus destroyed Jerusalem I made my way back to find rubble and grieving Jews, most of them enslaved. Among them were Jesus's followers, who'd formed one of many Jewish subcultures that sprang up as catastrophe closed in. For a while I thought these Christian Jews with their gentler doctrine might be on to something, although I was less than enchanted with Jesus's declaration: "he that loveth son or daughter more than me is not worthy of me." At least he never, as far as I could tell, instructed followers to go out and kill either their progeny or anyone else—a big improvement over the previous administration. But it didn't take long before Christians were murdering for Jesus anyway. Did it really matter what he said? Maniacs do what they want to do.

◆

"I'm not a hooker," Tony said, lightly caressing my ear.

"Who said you were?"

"It's what you thought though. How long's your boss gonna be on the phone?"

"Why? There something you need to do? Or maybe just something you *want* to do."

"This is kind of fun, isn't it? This big mansion." She slipped out of her boots, and after a few more mutually entertaining kisses I helped her slip out of her dress too, no more teasing. She wanted to penalize Trianon for falling asleep, and I was the beneficiary.

Tony had pixie breasts to match her pixie face and curls. A hint of a small tattoo, red and green, visible beneath her panty hose, well below her waist. I thought of Ruth's tattoo above her breast. I hated the damn thing. I'd give anything to see it again.

"What makes you think I'm so easy?" I said, pulling off my trousers.

"That," she said, pointing to the bulge in my underwear. I reached behind us and pulled down the bedding to reveal clean, crisp sheets. Their pleasing aroma.

"Are you crazy?" she said, speaking now *sotto voce*, as though she just remembered we ought to be careful. "They'll know." She reached out to restore the bedspread and blanket, but I caught her arm.

"So what?" I said.

"What about your boss though? He might say something. I'd lose my tip."

"He's a man of the world."

She bit her bottom lip and squinted, thinking it over, then slipped under the covers and out of her panty hose. "You *want* him to know, don't you? Trianon."

"And you don't?" I said, moving in.

"I just want— I don't know. The man's really a creep, isn't he?" She touched my dick. "Don't tell me you changed your mind." For a year now I'd had trouble keeping erections. She sat up suddenly, as though she had something important to share. "The scars," she said. "What're they from?"

"Iraq." This was both a lie and partly true. Sometimes I go to extraordinary lengths not to lie. You might call it an obsession that's based on my experiences with people who lie and people who don't. I can't bear to be in the wrong camp. In this case I had in fact spent time in Babylon, including war time, but the precise circumstance of each battle scar (most were from battle but there were also work scars, life scars) was something I'd failed to track.

"Thought so," she said, snuggling next to me. She fingered the bracelet around my upper arm but said nothing about it.

"I'll turn off the light," I said. "I look better in the dark."

"You're funny." She massaged my groin area, teasing me back to stiffness. Her own crotch was of course shaved. Such styles have long since ceased to amaze me. I've seen them all.

"Starting to like me again?" she said, pulling back the covers to nuzzle my dick. Her rock 'n' roll generation thought oral sex was barely personal and not terribly intimate. Another trend that comes and goes. Just then I hoped it wouldn't go away any time soon.

Everything was humming until she drew a condom from her purse and tried to slip it on my suddenly wilting member. She showed only mild disappointment. "Come on, let's go back."

I pulled her to me and kissed her full on the lips. She tried to pull away at first, then warmed to it. After that there was no more trouble.

❧

Dressed again, she stood back and surveyed the remade bed, then smoothed the bedspread with her flawless white hand. The fabric was a flowered print and probably cost as much as the scoreboard-sized TV screen in the room where we'd left Trianon.

Don't feel guilty, moron. You made a clean break with Ruth. She's with Anton Borges.

"Were you at Billy Blankenship's funeral?" I asked her.

She shook her head. Wrong blonde.

"Okay, you're not a hooker. But you said he's paying you. What are you then? A professional ornament?"

She tousled my hair. "Not exactly," she said, straightening my shirt collar. "Judy and me, we've been here before. He asked for us."

We found Trianon snoring still, head back, mouth open. The other blonde looked up from a Seinfeld rerun while Powell punched out a number on his cell. He shook his head at me to signal exasperation, but I could tell he didn't really give a damn that I'd gone off with Tony.

"What did you mean 'not exactly'?" I whispered to her.

"It's a secret," she whispered back, suppressing a laugh. Cell phone to his ear, Powell slipped out of the room again.

"Then you shouldn't have mentioned it," I told her in a soft but no longer whispering voice.

She murmured, "You won't tell Powell?"

"Promise."

"Won't tell anybody?"

"I swear." We were like old friends now.

She stared at Trianon, making sure he was asleep. "Look, it's kind of gross, okay?" she said, *sotto voce*. I shrugged to signal the wide boundaries of my tolerance. "He gives us each a big line of coke for down there." She looked down toward her knees. But she wasn't talking about her knees. The other blonde giggled.

"No, not there exactly," Tony whispered. She pulled her head back and to the side in a quick gesture, meaning behind her. She covered her mouth to suppress a laugh. "Then he snorts it out with a straw." Still grinning, she shrugged and said a little louder, "I know. Kind of icky."

"That's not what you told me," her pal Judy said.

"Stop listening, you creep." Tony picked up a throw pillow and tossed it at her playfully.

Powell entered at a fast clip. "We're going," he said.

"No, you're too late," Tony told me.

"For what?"

"To ask for my number."

"Come on," I said.

She shook her head no.

"I'll wake him up," I threatened.

"You don't really want it anyway."

"I will."

"Gimme a pen."

I found a financial magazine on an end table and tore off the back cover. She wrote out her number in a tiny scrawl followed by a smiley face. Then she cupped her hands over my ear and whispered into it, "I don't smoke either."

RUTH

I lived through two eras in New York—B.B. and A.B.—Before Ben and After Ben. Not even the book juggernaut had as much impact on my life as meeting him. A sensitive soul with quick wit and a cute lisp, he became my friend, my lifeline. Only five minutes after tripping over my cord he admitted doing it on purpose. "You were so diligent it was adorable. *You* were adorable."

Two weeks later he knew everything about me—from Lenny and Borges all the way back to my life in foster homes. And only three weeks into the A.B. era, I was staggered by a memory that predated the night at the carnival. It was Ben—not Lenny, not Evelyn nor anyone else—who managed to pull open a drawer I'd thought was locked forever. He didn't do it by asking questions. It was just his presence. You think you know yourself and then you discover you're carrying around secrets that some part of you won't reveal to another part. We're wired with greater complexity than our conscious mind can capture. I was just taking a bite of cheese and cracker when I realized what was happening. Ben looked at me quizzically as I held my forehead with both hands, afraid to chew.

When I was sure I couldn't remember any more, I described, blinking back tears, what I'd just seen. Slowly, just above a whisper. Ben told me later that he held his breath as I spoke in fear of breaking the spell.

I was on my back in a buggy, and my mother wheeled me under a shade tree, probably in our backyard. I couldn't make out her face, but it was the face of someone who cherished me. She spoke gently to me, bent down and kissed my eyes, which felt funny and very pleasant, and then she disappeared. I cried when I realized she'd gone, but I soon busied myself studying the leaves on the tree's branches. They were different colors and made a lonely, spooky sound rustling in the breeze. The light was dim there in the shade. I'm sure I fell asleep. When my mother returned I felt an ecstasy, I realized now, that I'd labored to duplicate ever since. She kissed me and smiled and there was a kind of music in her voice. The world was a fine place to be.

"What else?" said Ben in a half-whisper.

"I think— No, that's all of it. I can't see her face. If only I could see her face. Oh Ben."

Tears had formed in his pale blue eyes. "Such a precious memory," he said.

"Ben, she loved me. Why'd she let me go?"

"Maybe she died or was hurt. Maybe she became very ill. And whoever took you next, they're the ones who left you at the carnival. I bet it wasn't your mother at all. Don't you see? She did the best she could and never stopped loving you."

It took a while before I could speak. Then I said, "Ben, listen to me. You're my brother, father, something. I love you."

"Brother," he sniffed. "I love you too."

We hugged oh so tight.

◈

Ben had only one piece of advice regarding Lenny. "Call him in the middle of the night. Sometimes when people are sleepy enough, they tell the truth. Beyond that I just can't say without meeting him. But you're awfully levelheaded for a gorgeous celebrity. So if you're still thinking about him this much, I assume you have good reason. Still, it's all very puzzling."

"Ever make one of those middle-of-the-night calls yourself?"

"No, I'm too timid to take my own advice. I'm Walter Mitty's shyer, little brother—the kid who found *My Fair Lady* and his mother's eyeliner. But beneath this pitted, pudgy package there was a fairly nice man waiting to be unwrapped. I'm so happy you guessed that, Ruth."

"You're *not* pitted or pudgy. You're a handsome brute."

Ben wouldn't let me see any old photos, but apparently he really was pitted and pudgy before he hired physicians in Antigua to redo his exterior. Now, after all the plastic surgery, liposuction, hair plugs, and steroids, sixty-year-old Ben looked like a mildly artificial forty-two. Nothing they'd done to him jumped out at you. You just had a sense some of him was manufactured outside normal channels. I worried about all the chemicals they pumped into him, but he just joked that now he'd make a great-looking corpse. Periodically he'd return to Antigua for surgical touch-ups and "stuff," which I gathered meant steroid injections.

"One of the doctors—well, he isn't a *doctor* doctor, but he has this beautiful office way up in the hills. He gives you these tests to measure chemicals in your system. He tells me, 'You've got excellent readings for a man your age.' So I go, 'I don't want excellent readings for a man my age. I want excellent readings for a high school quarterback, understand? Fill 'er up.'"

"Are you sure this is even science?" I asked him.

"Gay science," he grinned.

Ben was a film editor in demand—almost exclusively for documentaries. He was also plugged into an enormous network of artistic and intellectual circles. I'd seen Robert De Niro greet him with a hug. Ben seemed to know everybody whose imagination and drive infused New York with an inquisitive perspective that extended even to the butcher who teased me for discussing Moses in my book without having read Martin Buber. After I checked out Buber I had to go back to his meat counter and apologize. "You'll get it right next time," he said. He was a magnanimous meat cutter.

Ben even had dirt on Columbia University's Exploratory Task Force. He's the one who filled me in on Jorge's sexual history. "But mostly," he said, "they're recluses over there.

They come out on Groundhog Day or something. The whole crew's a weird, weird bunch. Their scholars?—I think they call them scholars—*really* keep to themselves. Except for Borges, of course. But those clerks, they're so strange. The way they dress and— Even the straight males whisper like little girls. But listen, I can't believe you're not sleeping with him, Borges. Don't look at me like that. Smile if you really are. Kidding, just kidding. But why deprive yourself? The man's a world-class hunk."

Ben became my party date. Social functions were more fun with him whispering everyone's secret history in my ear. By this time I was declining virtually all invitations from TV producers prowling for talking heads. This made me an even bigger prize, though that wasn't my intention. I just didn't want to keep repackaging the same old snake oil like all those "intellectuals" traveling the media circuit who gradually become all hat and no cattle. I needed to get my ideas—my mind was bursting with them—into new books. Discussing them on TV first would drown them at birth.

"May I tell you something?" Ben said. "I warn you, you might not like it."

"No."

"Shut up and listen. Everybody thinks you're sleeping with Borges."

"Are you kidding?"

"That's why you were so popular in the beginning. Now of course you've *earned* your spurs, but at first everyone just wanted to ingratiate themselves with Borges. A be-kind-to-the-plaything sort of thing."

Shit.

No, I hadn't told Ben about the night I slept with Borges in Santa Monica. No one knew except Evelyn. What I've failed to mention is that Borges was more than just sexy as hell. He was a fantastic lay—a god of erections and sensitivity. But even though the physical sensations were otherworldly, they still fell short of sex with someone I *belonged* having sex with.

After I hit the best-seller list, Borges put on a full-court press to "expand" our relationship. "If I ever was your boss, and that's debatable, I certainly am no longer. We're colleagues, Ruth. Colleagues who spent a magnificent night together. You know it was. And here we are together again and you're so enchanting and our lives are so short."

"Life is short? Can't you do better than that?"

But we both knew he saved my life in so many ways. People go home together for a lot less reason than that.

CHAPTER 14

RUTH

At least once a week Ben took the train out to New Jersey to visit his nine-year-old son Wayne, who lived with his mother.

"Don't ask me the story, okay? It happened. And it's one of the greatest— It's *the* greatest thing that ever happened to me." That's how it went. He paid homage to Wayne's existence and cut off further discussion. I obliged.

One day in the same coffee shop where he'd tripped over my electric cord, it struck me that Ben's bipolar disposition had been at the wrong pole for several days running. "Come on, Ben. What's wrong? Spit it out."

"Nothing."

"I tell *you* everything," I lied.

He took a deep breath, then another. "Wayne's beginning to understand more about . . . me. Lately he barely speaks to me, stopped calling me Dad."

"What's he call you?"

"Nothing. It's like 'hey you,' you know? It hurts. I can't teach him any of the things a father's supposed to teach a son. The fact is—" He shook his head. "—he hates me."

"You can teach him plenty. You teach me. And I'm sure he doesn't hate you."

"He throws like a— They say he throws like a girl. The other kids, they tease him about it. A lot, I think. I'm not sure. I know he gets picked last. I was always picked last too. It breaks my heart. And stop trying to comfort me. I'm a gay man who had a son when he was fifty-one years old. Let me wallow in pain, okay? I deserve it."

"Come on, Ben. You've gotten through worse than this."

"Sure, *I* have, but it's different pain when your child suffers."

"Well, I feel bad for you, if that helps."

"Feeling bad *for* me doesn't help much. What helps is when other people feel bad, *period*. Then you say, hey, at least I don't have *her* troubles. If no one else were happy, life would be so much better, don't you think?"

A week later I was watching a police officer and a bread truck lady flirting just outside the coffee shop window. Standing close enough to touch them was a homeless man diligently poking through a trash barrel. Remarkable how invisibly these poor souls move among us, like ghosts. I looked up to see Borges smiling over the rim of my laptop. "Let me take you to lunch," he said. "Please."

I didn't ask him how he found me, but I was thirty blocks from his office. He'd behaved himself ever since that kiss in the Santa Monica deli well over a year ago. It struck me yet again that Borges was brilliant, handsome, successful, witty, circumspect, and had rescued me from academic Outer Mongolia. The homeless man was no longer in sight. I should have given him something, shared my luck with someone.

"Can you play baseball?" I asked Borges.

He was still standing, waiting for an invitation to be seated. I had him trained. "Come again?"

"Sit down," I told him. "Let's eat here. The sandwiches aren't too bad. Can you throw and catch and hit a baseball?"

"Of course," he said, sitting down. "I grew up in Louisiana."

"Louisiana? Where'd you get your FDR accent?"

"I'm a phony. Listen, I have news. You're now a faculty member, officially."

"Wonderful."

"Also, you've been awarded tenure as an associate professor."

"Impossible. I never *asked* for tenure."

"Oh, Sally took care of all that."

"But I'd have to do weeks of paperwork, and I never even signed anything or flattered any committee members. I didn't even know I *had* committee members. Are you sure about this?"

"At first we were shooting for your birthday, but your folder flew through all the stops, and we decided it would be unfair to make you wait that long." Only yesterday, it seemed, I'd been a factotum. And now? Now I was on the edge of tears. Borges sensed this, I'm sure, so he kept talking while I regained control. "It's so nice when academics can act like grown-ups," he said, referring to the committee members.

"Who forged my signature? Sally?"

"No."

"Somebody had to."

He flashed a rascally smile. "I thought if I carried the news in person I might earn a peck on the cheek. God, that was pathetic, wasn't it?"

"Yes."

"Wait a minute. You mentioned some baseball thing. What evil scheme are you hatching?"

"I'll get to that, but thanks, Borges, for not waiting for my birthday. Because then I'd have to murder you for keeping me in the dark and that would have ruined everything, practically." I leaned across the table and pecked him on the cheek.

My actual birthday, at least the precise date, was of course a mystery. I was found at the carnival on July 16th, and the doctors figured that was somewhere close to my second birthday. For years I'd wracked my brain trying to figure how a birthday anniversary might have related to my abandonment, but I never came up with anything that made sense. Later I had my date of birth officially set on Bastille Day, July 14th.

I told Borges I wanted a favor. "But it's just a favor. There's no scheme. I want you to teach a nine-year-old boy how to play baseball. And if possible, teach him not to despise his father for being gay."

"A tall order, but an honorable one. Where is this boy?"

"New Jersey. Around Hackensack, I think."

"Jesus Christ. What do I get in return for all this?"

"You get the satisfaction of doing a good deed." I leaned forward again and this time kissed him lightly on the lips. "We won't spell out the rest."

He placed his hand on my shoulder, but I moved back to my side of our little table. "First deliver the package," I said.

"You don't trust me?"

"I trust you some. But you must know your whole task force is weird, Borges. Except for you, I haven't met one other scholar. At the Christmas party it was me, you, and the fashion zombies."

"But it all works out, doesn't it? Professor Canby."

Professor Canby. I'd slaved and eaten dirt and traded years of my life to be Professor Canby. I'd still be in quicksand if it weren't for this man. I wrote down Ben's name and cell number and pushed it across the table. "This is the father. Explain you're going to help his son."

"Oh, Ben, of course. A lovely man. I'm glad to help. Except, do I really have to go out to Jersey? Not that you're not worth it."

"Maybe Ben or his mother can take him into the city. Work it out with them, okay? Besides, what's wrong with Jersey? You're from Louisiana, for Christ's sake."

"You're not going to use that against me, are you?"

"Every chance I get."

"What if the boy—"

"His name is Wayne."

"What if Wayne doesn't *want* to learn baseball?"

"He's dying to. Just charm him. I'll help if you like. But don't stalk me anymore, okay? I almost maced you."

"Stalk you? Here? Jesus, Ruth, don't you know you're famous? Everybody who reads the *Post* knows you hang out in this coffee shop."

"And I suppose you read the *Post*."

"I read anything that leads me to you. Okay, gotta run. I have to look for my old baseball mitt. Is he right- or left-handed?"

"Ask Ben."

"You know, Ruth, no one's ever made me jump through hoops the way you do. I love it."

He flew out the door like a twelve-year-old and never ate lunch. In three weeks Ben's kid would probably be the next Stan Musial.

Was it wrong to peddle my ass to help a friend? It sure felt like it. But it felt that way to Huck when he chose hell over Jim's slavery. Anyway, the fact that Borges and I already slept together once could be defined as an extenuating circumstance. And it seemed the whole world was conspiring to put us in bed together. Why did everyone have to make such a fuss about sex? Break it down and what is it? The touching and penetrating of body orifices. This flesh touches that flesh. What made it such a defining activity? Why did I feel so awful?

LENNY

I suggested Tony meet me at the same Farmers Market coffee shop where I'd first seen Ruth. But she had a better idea—the Polo Lounge. Okay, I said. Although I disliked being taken for a chump, I've never worried much about money except when I run out. I also figured that her brazen rapacity promised to simplify our relationship, making it more agreeable for both of us. Or at least so I hoped.

She went heavy on the perfume and wore a red, spangly dress so tiny it was a borderline misdemeanor. She barely looked at the menu, just told the waiter what she wanted. It was up to him to find it for her. Somewhere in her travels she'd learned to behave like a starlet. Her appetizer alone cost thirty-eight dollars. In fact, the bill was so enormous it gave me the first good laugh I'd had in a while. She slurped my dollars like a milkshake. And she was distant. I couldn't reconstitute the friendship we'd felt the first time. She didn't even care to try. I was a john now, and she had to punish me for it. Even the waiter seemed to sense the disaster unfolding at our table. At some point Tony looked at me with those hard whore eyes and showed me a photo of her boyfriend. "Isn't he cute?"

He had matted, wild-ass hair that stuck out Borneo head-hunter-style and wore a sleeveless t-shirt to show off arms covered in tattoos of spiderwebs and things. Behind him was the yellow dust of Babylon, where he was supposed to help build cell phone towers for some sleazy American contractor.

I took her straight home from the restaurant, and we kissed goodnight with the mutual understanding that we'd never see each other again.

That same week I accompanied Powell to the Super Bowl in San Diego. Not just for the game, which we'd see from a stadium skybox, but for three days of the world-famous, vulgar excess that surrounded it. This year he'd received entrée to the game and several of the more exclusive parties. "About time somebody opened up the parlor for a Detroit nigger," he said. Even though parties mostly bored him, clearly it had hurt him deeply to be left off the A-list all those years. As for me, I was curious to see twenty-first century bacchanalia, and I considered that curiosity a good sign. Malaise is dangerous. Stop caring long enough and something kills you.

It was only after we checked into our suite that I discovered Powell's platinum invitations had all come through Trianon. The parties were big, loud, and surprisingly uninspiring. All those splendid-looking women wandering around in their meticulous regalia just made me long for Ruth. Meanwhile we were besieged by drunks who wanted their picture taken with Powell. Two nights running we took refuge in our suite by eleven P.M. Powell didn't even bother to pick up any of the elaborate gift packages.

On game day our limo driver whizzed us through a special gate and took us to a parking spot beneath the stadium. A private elevator brought us straight to the glitter of Trianon's skybox. No need to mix with the rabble. A young woman with a clipboard and an Ivy League aura greeted us when the doors opened. There were generous sprinkles of celebrities. Some of them seemed to think fame gave them a license to bore everyone to death. Powell was cornered for almost ten minutes by a powerful congressman in a ginger hairpiece that looked like it came off the shelf of a drugstore chain. Trianon had acquired two brand new blondes in little black dresses.

Shortly before kickoff I was selecting lobster tail from the buffet when I heard gales of laughter. I looked up at Trianon's giant screen and saw me and Tony making love.

"Darn, where did that come from?" jested Trianon. Standing with the remote in his hand, he let the digital recording go on a tad longer before switching back to the pre-game show. "I do hope no one was offended," he said, which made everyone laugh even harder. I doubt they all connected me to the figures on the screen at first, but after a few minutes of round-robin whispering they did.

Earlier I'd noticed that Trianon had a security team of two steroidal off-duty cops packing pistols under their jackets. Police personalities have remained remarkably static down through the centuries and across continents, always attracting a plentitude of thugs. As Western governments became more responsive to their respective publics, the thugs learned to become more duplicitous, but their fundamental nature was basically unchanged. Jubal had scolded me more than once for working alongside a couple of cops who moonlighted on Zev's crew. A New York cop, he reminded me, had once battered Miles Davis—*Miles fucking Davis*—with a nightstick for conversing with a white woman between sets. "I like to think I'm a free man in a free country," Jubal once told me. "Cops, they like to prove I'm a deluded nigger."

Trianon approached with his customary glass of bright green liquid and a crooked smile on his hang dog face. "I threw that little whore in the street, you know," he said between sips.

"You must be very proud."

The response clearly annoyed him though he tried mightily not to show it. I wondered when her ejection took place—almost certainly before that night at the Polo Lounge, but Tony never said a word about it. I hoped it wasn't terribly ugly but knew it probably was.

"Don't you know there are cameras everywhere?" said Trianon. "And servants? They love to tattle. I thought about getting her fired from that come-stained sewer she works in, but I decided—you know what?—it suits her, the little cunt."

"Tony. Her name is Tony."

"If you say so."

His two cops watched me carefully and weren't afraid to show it. Their muscles bulged out of their clothes like fresh-popped bags of microwave popcorn. They were like the dodo birds that used to walk straight up to the men who slaughtered them. Maybe they thought misfortune wouldn't call without sending a postcard first. *No*, I told myself. *Mustn't go to jail.*

"I hope our little joke didn't disturb you," Trianon said.

"But evidently I disturbed you. You went to quite a bit of trouble."

"You know that Borges fellow?" Trianon said. "I hear he's fucking what's her name? That other bitch of yours. The writer. Maybe they're making tapes too. I'll see if I can get them for you." His head jiggled up and down in silent laughter that turned into a snort. "Suddenly you don't look so slick, Slick. Something bothering you?"

But I already knew about Anton Borges. And Trianon was a dead man anyway, as was everyone else around me with their pitifully short lives. All I had to do was wait a bit. I'd told myself that so many times when I thought someone needed killing. Just show a little patience and it will all be solved without my help. I looked at Trianon with his gleeful, sagging, wolf face and his two sullen cops, and I took in all the celebrities and hangers-on and idle rich surrounding us in his ridiculous San Diego skybox. They hungered for mayhem. Most mortals do. That's why they gather to watch football games.

Ruth was a grown woman, and I didn't expect her to remain celibate. Maybe this Borges person could bring her happiness. Still, I calculated the value of Trianon's life, and the results weren't in his favor. Lives are precious, but not, I'd long since concluded, sacred.

"She made a deal at the crossroads," said Powell, beside Trianon now.

What? What deal is this?

"You remember Borges," Trianon said. "He was at Blankenship's funeral. Tall fellow? Long blond hair? He seemed to frighten you, as I recall."

Powell: "Be cool."

- 144 -

I grabbed Powell by his lapels. "You've been watching me. For him."

"I told you once he's a good man not to know. Anybody who can do it, they should stay away from him. But she can't. Not anymore. Like I said, she made a deal at the crossroads."

A cop reached out a meaty hand to grab me.

CHAPTER 15

RUTH

Ben left my side to sidle through the chichi throng of party-goers and eventually reached Borges with a fanatical embrace. I watched them as Sharon Stone told me more about her I.Q. than I cared to know. My mind was mostly on Thorstein Veblen, the long overlooked Gilded Age economic philosopher who'd invented the term "conspicuous consumption" and viewed the capitalist barons of his day as mad creatures moving about in a vast diorama of the absurd.

I recalled reading that Ms. Stone had once used her celebrity connections to badger zoo officials into letting her hubby visit a Komodo dragon in his cage. Unimpressed by her film credits, the dragon bit off a chunk of hubby's foot. It struck me that a short interview with Ms. Stone might help me illustrate the enduring power of Veblen's analysis, but she took a call on her cell and next thing I knew I was pulled into a little circle with Borges and a French cultural minister with fantastic legs who was nevertheless a bit old for her short skirt.

Borges: "Ever wonder why our little Exploratory Task Force, unlike think tanks, ballparks, and stadiums, hasn't been named for anybody? Why it's not a Pepsi-Cola or a Toyota or a Pringles Potato Chips Task Force?"

"All right, Borges, why not?" the attractive Frenchwoman whose name I couldn't recall dutifully asked him teasingly. Another femme felled.

"Well"—he placed his empty wine glass on the tray of a passing purple-haired waiter—"everything may look placid on the surface, but beneath the waterline all the luminaries of legal tender are paddling their little duck feet like crazy. They'd love to put their name on it, and they know it's in play, but they can't figure out the right price. We respond to all queries with a flat no. Without comment. It drives them crazy. They're all narcissists and thieving industrialists, you understand."

"So why not just accept the highest offer?" I asked him.

"There *had* been a lull in the bidding, and I was beginning to think, well, maybe we better grovel back to the top bidder. But then we received an offer today, right out of the blue, that's *forty percent* above the last one. I'm going to let them drool just awhile longer, but I sense a top right here."

"You're a true renaissance man," said the Frenchwoman. "Both an artist and a swindler." She playfully tapped the tip of his nose with her index finger. I noticed an emerald bracelet you could use to signal other planets.

"It's one of my most rewarding hobbies," he said, "extracting dollars from dignitaries."

"A truly cunning ape," I pointed out, "doesn't beat his chest."

The Cabinet member gave me an appreciative smile, then pecked Borges on the cheek. "Such a *charming* ape though, don't you agree?"

Why would anyone bring up sums of money, center a discussion around it, yet conceal the amount? Because money is a sacrament, like the Lord's name that Orthodox Jews won't pronounce. Most people will give you more details about their sex lives than their paychecks. Or was I overreacting because Borges wasn't Lenny? Maybe I'd built Lenny into a god that didn't really exist. But wouldn't it be lovely to have him back for just a little while?

"Ruth!"

"Hmm?"

"Return to our hemisphere, please."

"Sorry, I was thinking, Borges. According to you, it's what I'm paid to do."

"That and other things. Aimée's gone to the john. Would you like to know whose name is going on the Task Force?"

"Not particularly."

His features remained playful, but I'd wounded him back for his "other things" remark.

"Trianon. Arthur Trianon. Tell no one, of course."

"Afraid I don't know who he is."

"Exactly. He thinks everyone should know who he is, and he's willing to pay for the privilege."

"The— What's his first name?"

"Arthur."

"The Arthur Trianon Institute?"

"Precisely."

"Catchy," I said.

"Bitchy tonight, aren't we?"

"Where are the other scholars, Borges?"

"Working, I imagine. They're an industrious group. As you well know. Rasmussen's book will get a two-page spread in *Vanity Fair*. And we'll see from there."

"Great. But where's Rasmussen? What the fuck is going on?"

"How would you like to do something special tonight?"

"I could allude to it, you know, these puzzling Task Force scholars who might or might not exist. In an article or an interview. I could even devote an entire piece. 'The Missing Scholars of Manhattan.' Should I write it before or after we become the Alex Trianon Institute?"

"Arthur, dear. His name is Arthur. The poor schlub deserves at least a modicum of accuracy. He and his fellow schlubs pay our salaries, after all." He rested both arms on my shoulders, touching my ears with his fingers and whispered, "Darling, Aimée has a 1979 Petrus Bordeaux at her hotel. Ever try a thousand-dollar bottle of wine?"

"Every Saturday night in Arizona."

"Well, then you can relive old times. Incidentally, she's mad about the little tortoise over your breast. She's dying to see more."

"Why do I always do what you want? I don't even like you."

"Dear Ruth. I do hope those tears are for joy. Anticipatory joy." He spoke now like a man gentling a horse.

LENNY

"You must be a fighter," Powell said. "How come I never heard of you?"

"Cut the bullshit."

"Bullshit? I'll give you a contract right now."

In the twenties I had in fact competed as a welterweight in Berlin. I was pretty good, but not as good as Powell pretended or at least wanted to believe. People are always willing to regard someone or something they don't have as superior to whomever or whatever they're tired of. We'd sent his driver back to the hotel and taken a tram to downtown San Diego, where we now sat in a Denny's booth. I was nursing a banged up ear—a souvenir from the Hispanic cop who grazed me with his sap. It would turn cauliflower if I didn't get it drained.

"Do you know who I am?" I asked him.

"Told you. I never heard of you."

"What did . . . Borges. What did Borges tell you about me?"

"I'll tell you everything I know, which is not much. Don't look at me like that. You *know* this man we're talking about. How much he tell you? That's what he tells me, too. Anyway, where you get off getting mad at *me*? Working for me you just punched out two cops and hung a man who's way richer than I am up on a hook like a slab of meat. I can already smell the lawsuits cooking. But since there's just us two here, let me tell you, what you did to Trianon?" He broke into prolonged, hearty laughter so infectious that if it weren't for Ruth, I'd have laughed too. Every minute I spent sitting on the wrong coast was agony. But I had a better chance of helping her if I went out there armed with information.

"You see the look on his face? Hanging up there by his collar? Looked like a—"

"Like a trapped wolf," I said.

"That's it. That's it exactly. A real ugly one though."

"What was the deal you made with Borges?"

His eyes still looked in my direction, but they were on something no one else could see. After awhile, he said, "I was just out a stir. Jobs? Weren't no jobs. Not for niggers or ex-cons, and I was both. Finally I got hold of an old piece, nickel-plated an' all rusted inside. Probably woulda exploded on me if I pulled the trigger. One night I stick up this white man in downtown Detroit. Least I tried to stick him up. Cause he just laughed at me. 'You can't be messing around with these penny-ante scores,' he says. 'You'll just wind up back in the joint. You should be stealing big-time. Less chance a getting caught.'

"The man knew everything about me, and there was not a speck of fear. Nothing. Something here's not right, I tell myself. I rest the barrel right on his nose. No change. Scared me instead a him. Now I just want to get outa there. I'd a given the man *my* watch if I had one. Well, he puts an arm around my shoulder, takes me over to a fancy restaurant. There I am, a street nigger in shabby clothes. This cat must be crazy, right? I just want to get out of there, but sure enough, they give us a table, just the one he asks for. Everything he wants, they bring it, smiling like motherfuckers, like I was the mayor or something. They bring over a sport jacket to cover my funky shirt, then we get these big steaks, and next thing I know he's set me up to run this boxing show. It's a fund-raiser for some health clinic. Me? Organize a boxing card? You can do it, he says. He had— The man knew I could. Just like that, he knew. I walked away with forty thousand from that show and never looked back."

"So what did you do for him?"

"He never spelled it out."

"And you made the deal anyway? Doesn't sound like Ray Powell."

"I had the right pigmentation, I could be running GE. Run it better, too. You ever think a that?"

"Funny thing is, I did."

"'We know little of the things for which we pray.' Chaucer."

"When did you first meet this Borges?"

"Long time," he said. "It's been a long time."

"You're what? Seventy-two, seventy-three?"

"Seventy-five."

"You've been in the boxing business, what? Forty years?"

"About that."

"So the night you tried to stick up Borges he was maybe two or three years old."

After a pause, Powell said, "He was a different guy. The same, but different. You know what I'm talking about."

"So who is he really?"

"I try not to think about it. Who do *you* think?"

"Who helps a man steal forty thousand dollars from a charity?"

"I know what you're saying. Believe me. I know. But I still got hope. We donate to things, causes. My wife and me." He said this testily, assuming I'd disbelieve his generosity. "Let me ask you something. When you have to take a plane somewhere, you fly coach?"

I nodded impatiently, but he stopped me before I could interrupt.

"And you board way up front where you got to slink past all those business-class motherfuckers to find your itty bitty seat in back. Maybe they pretend not to notice you. Or maybe they look right *at* you, like, look at *that* dumb motherfucker. Can't afford a man-sized seat. You ever wonder why they make the planes like that? Putting all the losers on a walk of shame?"

"Most people go past first-class without worrying about it," I said.

"'Cause you don't want to know, don't want to *think*. But me, I don't fly coach. Ain't shinin' *no* man's shoes."

Flying coach was infinitely superior to bouncing around on an oxcart. Unlike Powell, unlike so many others, I didn't lust for more, for an unobtainable satiety. I floated aimlessly like the rest of them, but free of that particular madness. Give me another four thousand years and I might even learn a little more.

"What'd he tell you about me? Borges?"

"It was maybe a forty second conversation. 'Do me a favor,' he says. 'Keep this guy close. I'll get in touch later.' He never did. And believe me, I don't ever go looking for him."

"How's Trianon figure in this?"

"Borges has a deal with him, too. I think. We don't talk about it."

"But Trianon knew something about Ruth. What about you? What do you know about her and Borges?"

"I knew you once had something going with Ruth Canby. From what Trianon said, I figured she made the same deal I made, Trianon made. The deal at the crossroads. I read her book, you know. She writes like the devil."

Feeling a chill is a metaphorical expression. But I wasn't feeling an expression. I felt a chill. "Got any money?" I asked him.

He reached inside his jacket, pulled out a roll, and tossed it on the table. "You're a better stick-up man than I ever was."

It was about four hundred. I gave him back two twenties. I didn't know whether anyone had filed a report back there at the stadium, but the two cops might want revenge badly enough to embarrass themselves further. Who was I kidding? It would be up to Trianon. Which meant it would be up to The Beast.

"He knows you're coming. You know that."

I knew that.

I sold my ten thousand-dollar car to Jubal for all he had, eight hundred. He'd offered to send more later, but I told him to forget it. I asked him to clean out my apartment. "Tell the landlord first," he said. "He calls Manhattan Beach cops and they see a nigger carrying out a TV, that nigger better be Barack Obama."

I was practiced at this, leaving friends behind.

"Don't guess we'll be seeing you for awhile," he said.

"You never know. Maybe some jazz joint in hell."

He grinned. "That ear. How's it figure in this?"

"There's no time to go into it."

"Get it fixed. You know Pamela said, 'I think Lenny's on the lam.' Said that first time she met you."

"Give her my love."

Maybe I'd gotten sloppy. Or maybe Pamela was one of those sensitive souls I ran into from time to time, the oracles and seers. She and Jubal were proof that life is worth living. Someone else like them might come around the next corner. But if I couldn't get Ruth past this calamity, what difference would it make?

CHAPTER 16

RUTH

I knew how terrible I looked. Of course he didn't mention it, but it probably caused some of the worry in his eyes. *Damn his eyes.*

"Please go away," I said.

"I've got things to explain," Lenny said.

"It doesn't matter anymore."

How long had he been waiting outside my building? What's the difference? I headed off toward the little grocery on the corner. He tagged along uninvited.

"I *have* to explain it. You'll see why later. But first you'll think I'm crazy."

"I don't care if you're crazy or not. Just leave me alone."

"I've been standing out here three days. Almost around the clock."

"I told you once. When the conversation is over, it's over."

"But we haven't had a conversation."

At that moment, the only person I hated more than Lenny was me.

"Goddamnit, don't follow me inside."

He waited outside the store like a dog while I raced through the narrow aisles, trying to get it over with and back to where I could breathe. Croissants, cheese, cereal. When in doubt, I threw it in my basket. I should have just called in the order, but my mind was only partly functional. I paid up and there he was, waiting next to the metal vending boxes of publications advertising sex and real estate.

"What about your groceries?" he said, tagging along again.

They deliver, schmuck.

"My real name isn't Lenny."

"Jesus fucking Christ! You didn't even tell me your real name? Will you just— Get away from me. Go!"

I walked faster now. I was nearly at my building. He stopped me, clutching both my arms. I tried to squirm away. He was too strong. I dug my nails into his forearms, but he didn't seem to notice. "Borges isn't who you think he is," he said.

"You want me to call a cop? I will."

"Listen to what I'm saying. Your life depends on it. Borges isn't who—"

"Right. He isn't who I think he is, you aren't who you said you were, and maybe I'm not who you think I am, either. Now leave me alone."

"Let me come up."

I shook my head, exasperated with my tears, and with him for waiting too long to find me.

"Let's walk over to the park then. Please. I still love you, Ruth. Never stopped."

"You love who I was, who you thought I was."

I wiped tears with my hand. He let go of my arms and handed me a handkerchief. I let him steer me past my building toward Central Park down the street. I don't know why.

"Will they deliver your groceries?"

"What's the difference?"

"You look kind of thin."

"I look like shit. Say it."

Except for the swollen, red ear I refused to ask him about, he looked wonderful, particularly for a man who'd been waiting out on the sidewalk for three days.

"The doorman will take care of the groceries," I said.

"Same guy who wouldn't let me go up?"

"*One* of the guys who wouldn't let you up." He'd tried more than once, but I wouldn't let them call the police.

We were inside the park now. He stopped at a bench along the path. "Okay here?"

Just to be disagreeable, I moved on to the next bench. I still hated us both, but I loved this park. I loved the ornate, elegant buildings along Central Park West. They lifted the spirits of anyone who allowed them to. I was almost glad to be outside again.

"He's using you to get to me," Lenny said. "When he's done he'll probably kill you unless I can stop him."

Oh Jesus. Lenny, Lenny, what's become of you? "Stop who?"

"Borges."

"And just how long has Borges been out to get you?"

"Look, if you're talking paranoia, everybody's not out to get me. Just him."

"How long? How long has this gone on?"

"A long time."

"Since before we met?"

"Yes."

"But I knew Borges *before* I knew you," I said. "A year before. Think about it. How could he have known we'd meet in Farmers Market that day? Your story makes no sense. Besides which, Borges doesn't go around killing people. You're all mixed up. Don't you see that?" I got up, still clutching the handkerchief. "Thanks for the warning. I guess you're trying to help, but you're also— Lenny, you're sick, understand? You need help and you should get some. Please get some. But if you don't stay away I'll call the cops. I'm not kidding. And get the ear taken care of too. Do that right away."

I saw tears forming in his eyes. I wanted to put my arms around him. I didn't, and his lips moved as if to form a word. He took a deep breath. "My name is Yitzhak Ben Avraham. Isaac, son of Abraham. I'm *that* Isaac. Do you understand? *The* Isaac."

Oh my God. "Lenny, I'm sorry. I am. But I have to go." The earth, where so much had gone wrong for me, refused to swallow me; so I got up and headed toward my building, but of course he stayed with me.

"I know, I know. It sounds crazy. I wouldn't believe it either if I hadn't lived it. But I had to let you know. He must have had you in his back pocket all this time, and I was too stupid to see it. I saw it in dreams, but I paid no attention. You suffer in my dreams, and I stand there and do nothing. This went on for a long time and I didn't connect the dots, understand? My mind is so crowded with memories it doesn't always work as it should."

"I don't understand everything you're saying, but I do love you, Lenny. Or maybe I just love you for what we felt before. And I wish to God you weren't so ill. But we're finished. *You* finished us, and we can't— I don't hate you for being sick. I want you to get help, but I'm in no condition to help anyone right now." I stopped and hugged his steely frame, hugged hard, hanging on to my Lenny. He nuzzled my hair.

A group of preadolescents passed us. "Get a room," one of them hooted, and they all roared. They didn't spot our tears. We stepped back.

"How'd you get that ear?"

"Forget it. It's nothing. . . . He probably offers you things. Tantalizing things. But don't make deals with him. If you already accepted anything— I'll figure something out. Look, I'm the reason you suffer. I see that now, but I don't know how to make you understand this. It's the truth that's crazy. Not me."

"I heard what you said. Isaac. *The* Isaac. But I've read the bible, Lenny. And it says Isaac died." I went through a religious stage in high school, hoping to replace my latest set of shitty foster parents with Jesus, Mary, and Joseph.

"The bible also says the earth is less than six thousand years old and that man was created on the fifth day. Do you believe that or fossils and carbon dating?"

"Lenny, oh Lenny. You say you're a bible character and then you say don't believe in the bible. Isaac is . . . a fable. But even if there ever *were* an Isaac, he's— It's like saying you're King Arthur or a son of Zeus."

He rolled up his sleeve to reveal the antique band around his biceps. "It was from my mother. I know it doesn't prove anything. As far as I can figure out, I'm a bad joke. An old joke, I guess. Spared and forgotten. I don't bring any messages. Voices don't speak to me . . . nobody tells me anything. Understand? I just am. I spent days rehearsing this for you, and it's all—I screwed it up. So I'm just—" He shook his head.

I resumed walking, slowly this time, trying not to alarm him. No sudden movements. He stayed with me. Maybe I'd take a sleeping pill when I got home. I'd been trying to wean myself off them because my dreams were so terrifying now, but I loathed being awake.

"Think back to the person you used to be," I said. "Before you believed all this. Will you try to do that for me?"

"I wish I could get through to you."

"Okay, what happens if you get run over by a cement truck? Do you die and spring back to life? Do you heal or go on living all squished?"

"I get killed. Just like anybody else."

"How do you know?"

"I just do."

"Maybe you don't know as much as you think you do. Have you told anyone else about this?"

"No one."

"Not in all those years? Centuries? Millennia?"

"No."

"Why not?"

"I wasn't supposed to."

"How did you know that?"

"I just knew."

"So why tell me?"

"Because I have to help you."

"Show me a miracle, then."

"I'm the only miracle I know about. And . . . you call him Borges. I guess you could say he's a miracle. I always called him The Beast."

Watching my face, he looked more desperate, like he had to convince me so he could convince himself. I was out of questions. There was no point.

"I've seen him several times over . . . years. Many, many years."

I could no longer pretend Lenny was off somewhere living the sweet life to which he was entitled, but at least in some ways his illness was harmless, like a cartoon character who thinks he's Napoleon. It led him into making foolish choices, but he was largely functional. In fact, though crazy, he was too decent to be hooked up with a person like me, someone he was only trying to protect. I could have used protection, too, maybe a month ago, but our timing had always been off. We'd been run over by his insanity and my self-loathing, and now it was too late for us both. I worried about that ear. Who did he fight with? What had he done? I hated seeing him in physical pain.

Outside my building again, I clutched the metal railing next to the basement steps. It was something solid. "Look, Lenny, don't try to protect me from Borges. It's not— I'm not in danger and I don't want you arrested or anything, okay? Go home. Please. If I need help, I'll call. I promise." I pecked him on the cheek.

"Don't treat me like I'm nuts. You know me, Ruth. This is real. He knows I'm here, and if I leave— It's the worst thing to do. I don't want you—" He paused, blinking his eyes and licking his lips, both brand new tics, "—sacrificed."

"I'm listening to you, Lenny. I am. You're telling me you're Isaac and that Borges is some kind of devil. Maybe *the* devil."

"Maybe. I don't know. I've seen him do ugly, ugly things. I've also seen him . . . do kind things. But you can't count on kindness. I don't really know how he figures in anything, but I know I'm in his sights. And now you are too. You *are* suffering, aren't you? You don't deny it. In my dreams I see you in torment, you can't break free. It's you and him, sometimes others. I can't bear it. It's all my fault."

"I'm going in, Lenny. I have to. Get the ear taken care of, okay?"

"Don't blame yourself!" he shouted after me. "It's not you!" I entered the lobby and stole a quick glance behind me. He looked like a man who'd just missed the last train home.

The mystery of him, aching and awful though it was, had been easier to accept than the answer to that mystery. But a part of me couldn't help wondering whether he *had* spotted something real and terrible through his schizophrenic haze. Now, in addition to everything else, I had him to worry about too. We'd each gone our separate ways and wound up in adjoining rooms in hell.

Evelyn called every twenty minutes. Pleading messages. My nerves couldn't take it. Finally I picked up.

"At last. Look, Ruth, has Lenny showed up over there?"

"Yes."

She asked to speak to him, but I didn't know where he was staying.

"Does he know the police are looking for him back here?"

"No, yes, I don't know. Oh crap! Damn it. What happened? What'd he do?"

"Ruth, are you crying?"

"No, it's this damn cold." Followed by silence, Evelyn's way of telling me I'd just lied to her. "What happened? What'd he do?"

"Evidently he assaulted some people. . . . Ruth? You okay?"

"I'm okay."

"You don't sound so okay."

Where did this practice originate? Asserting that everything's coming up roses even as you're swept into the darkness?

And Evelyn wasn't being rhetorical either. She wanted the truth. But I wouldn't give it to her.

Two detectives looking for Lenny had showed up at the agency where he worked. They asked a lot of questions. The agency contacted friends of Lenny who also happened to know Evelyn.

"It sounded like the police were taking this very seriously," Evelyn said. She wanted him to turn himself in before it all got worse. One plague after another. I explained that Lenny was confused and hurt.

"Confused how?"

"Evelyn, please, I can't go into details right now. He's sick. He thinks he's someone else. That covers it."

"Look, when you see him again, hang on to him while we figure this thing out."

"But you don't like Lenny."

"He kind of grew on me. I just never told you. Look, what's the deal? When will you see him again?"

"I don't know." I was ashamed to admit I hadn't let him upstairs.

"I gave him your address. I'm sorry if it was awkward for you."

"Forget it. I just don't want him to hurt someone else—or himself."

"Ruth, you don't sound so good. You want me to come out there?"

"I'm okay. Really."

"Remember, it only hurts when you laugh."

"Then I'll be in great shape."

"You know," she said, "we haven't heard his side. Maybe the assault or whatever it was isn't as bad as it sounds."

"I know." She didn't understand that his side was pretty much moot now that he considered himself a fictitious bible character, but I couldn't bear to explain that.

"Lenny was evasive," Evelyn said, "but he was never a liar."

"I wonder if you could find out more about this—whatever happened, the incident back there. See if there's a warrant, or what?"

"That's a good idea. I don't know how, but I'll figure it out, okay?"

She would, too. That was her job. Solving problems, figuring things out.

"If you learn more," I said, "call. Night or day. What he needs is a doctor. Jail would be so stupid. I could scream." She offered again to come to New York. "You can be more helpful there," I said, and it was possibly true.

"Love you," Evelyn said.

I could only guess what it must be like to have a sister, but probably it felt like this. "Love you too," I said.

◈

"Look, the first thing you have to do—and this is so important— is protect yourself," Ben said. "I mean physically. This man is dangerous, Ruth. I'm sorry about your broken heart, but first things first. Don't let him hurt you or whatever it is his voices tell him to do."

We were drinking martinis. After we polished off the bottle of champagne he brought over, he went into the kitchen and using what he said was James Bond's recipe, he mixed a big pitcher from bar ingredients I'd inherited with the apartment. I'd never had a martini. It seemed like a good time to start.

"He's not dangerous, Ben. You don't know him."

"*I* don't know him? *You* don't know this guy. I bet you've spent more time with your dentist."

"Ben, I know you're trying to help, but don't refer to Lenny as 'this guy,' 'this man,' or any other dehumanizing terms. Please."

"Sorry."

Ben had come over to celebrate. He was flying off in the morning to edit his first Hollywood feature. I let him go on about his happy news awhile before I rained all my hapless, sorry crap on his parade. The film's budget wasn't huge, but it had a couple of recognizable names. "I smell a hit," he said, bouncing a little on the sofa. "I really do. Trouble is, I'm petrified. He's a genius, but this is one of the nastiest directors in Hollywood, in the *world*. He fires people. Right in front of everybody. Can you imagine? I couldn't stand it. I'd die."

"Don't worry about it. He wants a good movie, doesn't he? So he'll love you."

Throughout his career Ben had everyone convinced that documentaries were his preferred medium, but as he'd informed me early on, that was malarkey. "To work steady in documentaries, you have to take the documentary sacraments, take the vows. It's like you can't admit you're really hoping to get into a classier church."

Ben wanted me to call the cops on Lenny, but I assured him I was in no danger.

"What about Borges though? What if *he* has to pay the price? Or someone else? Once it starts— Oswald didn't just kill JFK. He murdered a cop too. That's how it works. Once they lose it, no one's safe."

Would it really be so awful if someone—not Lenny, but someone—were to rid the earth of Borges? Lenny, battered about in the maelstrom of his madness, might have stumbled into a righteous cause. They said there was always a foundation of truth upon which paranoids built their delusions.

"I'll explain it to Borges," I told Ben. "Now you go off to Hollywood and break a leg, but leave me your martini recipe."

"I read a newspaper column that said a good martini is like family. It's comforting. Don't worry, sweetheart. I'll be back."

"And use condoms," I said.

"It's not that kind of trip. I'll be working my ass off. Listen, did you warn them downstairs about Lenny?"

"They don't just let people up, Ben. You know that."

"Let's say goodbye down here on the couch," he said. "It'll be fun. Like necking."

"Jerk." We did the three-kisses routine followed by a protracted hug. He figured the job would take about six weeks. "Unless I get fired."

"Cut it out."

I called Borges right away, but he laughed it all off. "I'll keep one eye open for your abandoned lover, Ruth. But I'd like to sit down with you about your Veblen project if I could. It's just so damn exciting."

"Lenny did the abandoning. Not me."

"That settles it. He's crazy. Look, I'm in the middle of some things, but I'll be extricated soon. Why don't you jump in a cab?"

"I'm beat. How about meeting for coffee in the morning?"

"Ditch the hermit routine, okay? I'll send out for sushi, and we can pop the cork on that Château LaBalle."

"I'd rather not, Borges."

I started getting ready even as I resumed crying. Hiding in my apartment hadn't helped. Seeing Lenny hadn't helped. Chasing him away hadn't helped. Nothing helped.

Just before I stepped out the door I got another call from Evelyn.

"You said Lenny thinks he's someone else?"

"Yes."

"Well he *is* someone else. Leonard Hastings died two weeks after he was born in Chicago. Lenny, or whoever Lenny really is, stole his identity."

"But Lenny's from Israel. And how do you know this anyway?"

"The San Diego cops figured it out when they put out a warrant for his arrest. Lenny's got this friend Pamela who got it from somebody she knows inside the LAPD. And that's not all."

"What else?"

"They relayed all the information to the New York cops. They know he was headed out your way and they're treating this like he's Dillinger."

"All right. Thanks."

"Did you hear what I said?"

"I'll talk to you later, Evelyn. Gotta go."

Lenny's actions were being governed—and may have been for a long time—by his delusion that he was a supernatural being. Measured against that, the fake identity was a small concern. Now they'd punish him for his delusion. But weren't we all *taught* to accept delusions as real? Right from the start. Santa Claus, the Easter Bunny, one nation under God . . .

As I paid the fare, the cabdriver pretended I hadn't cried all the way to Rockefeller Center so I pretended too. I tried to tell myself this was only a bad dream, and I half believed it. It's only now, reliving the memory of it, that I know it wasn't.

CHAPTER 17

LENNY

Fear of spiders, snakes, heights, closed spaces—these are largely irrational phobias. But I couldn't categorize my fear of The Beast. I had no way of knowing whether my instincts were absurd, or, like the impulse to escape flames, perfectly reasonable.

And now, after four thousand years of keeping my secret, I'd finally revealed it to someone, and gotten precisely the result I'd expected. What Ruth failed to realize is that it would be a blessing of sorts if I *were* crazy. Crazy people sometimes lead quite tolerable lives. They can even star on Fox News.

Now Ruth was sinking in a mysterious swamp, and only I could see it. Maybe that meant I was crazy, but I'd leap in after her anyway. No more standing motionless while the victim is suffering torture. No more lethargy, indecision, cowardice, a compulsion to avoid attention, and all the other foolish behaviors that can prevent a man from doing what's right. Were I to freeze again, what purpose would I have left? To live another day. Like a lizard or a parrot.

But it's easier to see the wisdom of overcoming a phobia than to actually overcome it. Besides, was there really anything I could do to deter The Beast from whatever he was set on doing? I was in unfamiliar territory with no map, no mentor, no plan. I'd go in without one. Infantry soldiers have done that since the beginning of armies. To learn what's ahead, they move forward and find out. For centuries I'd evaded death, watching it silence one dissatisfied customer after another. Now I might have to accept it at last.

RUTH

Eleven years after Veblen's masterful The Theory of the Leisure Class *appeared in 1899, Norman Angell, a Laborite in the British Parliament, came out with* The Great Illusion, *a celebrated book arguing that in the modern trading economy, war no longer made sense and had therefore been rendered obsolete. You couldn't argue with his logic. But the Great War erupted only four years after the release of his book, turning Angell into a forgotten clown. Mankind could no more turn away from xenophobic, homicidal violence than it could suspend the deranged greed of the Gilded Age that was skewered so thoroughly by Veblen and Samuel Clemens.*

Marx, like Angell, considered himself a realist. So he assumed it was only a matter of time before the dispossessed multitude would topple the last mad tycoons and come together to share a pleasant, generous economy. But neither Veblen nor Clemens made the mistake of assuming humans would behave rationally. Understanding the terrible power of vile instinct, they, not Angell or Marx, were the realists.

—Notes by Ruth Canby

❖

I was trying to make sense of my notes when a nondescript man showed up at the next table, unpacked his laptop, and began to sigh. Every two or three minutes, like Old Faithful. I'd wait for the next one like a seasick passenger anticipating another dip of the vessel. I wondered what he saw on his laptop screen that was so aggressively lamentable. And just who was this upstart who dared to compete with everyone else's misfortune? Weren't we all suffering? Maybe he was a messenger from my own heart.

◈

I was desperate to get some clothes on, but I knew Borges would disapprove. He demanded we coat the grotesque nature of our relationship—which lately was being played out in the private suite adjoining his office—with smiles and false intimacy.

I'd tried to warn him a second time about Lenny, but it only resulted in another round of sex. He was utterly unconcerned, just as he'd been when confronted by Billy Blankenship and his bodyguard. Expressing my feelings to him took nearly all my fortitude, but he managed to turn them into something absurd, as though I were a bug trying to work a crossword puzzle.

"But he's telling me preposterous stories—that he has strange dreams and— I think he may be ill. I'm trying to ease him back to L.A. There's nothing for him here."

"That makes sense," Borges said.

"I loved this man, Borges. Love him still."

"I'm so sorry for the anguish it must cause you. But everyone has strange dreams. It doesn't mean he's ill, darling. Just what are these preposterous stories?"

When he called me "darling" or its equivalent, the word pierced me like a rusty nail. I ignored his question, so he followed it with another that was equally insincere:

"Is there anything I can do?"

"Yes, don't let him hurt you, but don't hurt him either."

"Engaging in brawls is not part of my ethos, darling. Anyway, should I run across him, I'm sure I can reason with him. Just an instinct of mine. Now, how's your Veblen project coming? Something tells me you haven't been toiling away in your little coffee shop."

Your little coffee shop. So much of what he said might or might not have a malicious double meaning. I pretended there was nothing odd about his knowing that I'd been neglecting my work, but precisely how did he know? When he pressed me on my Starbucks truancy I explained that a neurotic customer had driven me away.

"And you just let him?"

"What was I supposed to do? Explain I've been in *People* magazine?"

"You're too beautiful to be so cynical, darling."

I was well aware that if I could, as he suggested, manage to concentrate on my work again, there was a chance I'd gain at least an occasional recess from what had turned into a relentless misery. But my newly acquired writer's block was like the start of a cold. Impossible to know how long it would last. In the meantime, whenever I tried to assemble my thoughts into some kind of useful analysis they turned to scattered junk. I'd rewrite the same paragraphs over and over and watch them grow weaker instead of stronger.

New York, Borges pointed out, offered more than one coffee shop.

"I liked the one I had."

"The regularity of a habit is generally in proportion to its absurdity." He knew Proust, the bastard. And I remembered Lenny, something he'd said about Proust, something so endearing I nearly melted. Now look at me. "Or you could work at home," Borges said, and I was hearing him again. "Work here. Use your office. Use this suite. The library. We need you, darling. Share your genius. Now tell me, have you thought of incorporating Angell into your work?"

"No." I had tried another coffee shop, but a disheveled person of uncertain gender was playing a violin on the patio, going head to head against the abominable "world music" spilling from speakers inside and out. No one else seemed to notice the raging cacophony. At the library I found another nest of disturbances, including a patron who audibly swallowed her own snot. It was hell, a hell of my own making and there-fore a purer hell than the one Joseph Heller detected at the Port Authority Bus Terminal. I recalled Heller's *Picture This*, which pointed out that ancient Athens, so frequently cited as the birthplace of democracy, was in fact a society based on war and slavery, that its rapacious rulers must have been mad. As mad as Mohamed Atta at the controls of Flight 11 or corpo-rate plutocrats amassing their pointless plunder. As mad as the Arthur Trianon Institute.

◆

Nude, Borges rose from bed to brew a pot of coffee in the dimness of the kitchen area. He was a fan of chic blends and eso-teric coffee recipes. Thanks to his star persona, even baristas who had no idea who he was treated his detailed demands as though they were collaborating on a cancer vaccine. He could drink the concoctions any time of night and still sleep like a lamb.

As soon as he'd turned his back I pulled the sheet around me, hiding some of my nakedness. "What's the matter, dar-ling? Cold?" We watched each other as I let it fall. If I didn't make an issue of it, eventually he'd allow me to put on one of his robes. I made a mental note to bring my own next time so I wouldn't have to wear his next to my skin.

Eventually I realized that Borges, his teeth gleaming even in the faint light of his aquarium, was now referring to the miscalculations in Angell's thesis. "He could have saved him-self from studying those economic formulas if he'd just sat on a bench in Hyde Park and watched humanity. At some point he might have noticed that people are fucking crazy."

"Not people," I said, looking straight at his nude form as he turned to face me. "Men. Men are puny. They try to compensate for it with malice."

"Exactly," he said. "That's why, in the face of all that mad-ness, you, Ruth Canby, fire us with such lust. Your mind is an art that commingles with your physical beauty. It makes you even more than the astronomical sum of your parts, like nothing on Earth."

He leaned over the bed and kissed me on the mouth, then walked to the desk and picked up the phone. "Jorge, come in, please."

LENNY

I was prepared to do whatever was necessary to get past security at Rockefeller Center, but first I'd try to bluff my way in. I bought coveralls, packaging materials, and, to ice the cake, a clipboard. In the IDF they used to say that a soldier with a clipboard in his hand could obtain the nuclear launch codes. I also counted on the fact that New Yorkers, though they hate to be seen as gullible, love to do whatever feels cosmopolitan. That includes not being fazed by an urgent package delivery at eleven-fifteen P.M. When I casually but firmly insisted on a signature from the addressee, the security people in the lobby called upstairs, and, to my amazement, someone there agreed to let me up.

The imposing double doors leading to the Arthur Trianon Institute were just a few steps off the elevator. From what I could gather, the institute suite took up an entire floor. There was no bell, so I knocked. If no one came within five minutes I'd set off the fire alarm. I'd almost reached my deadline when a door finally opened. Standing there was a muscleman who strongly resembled a blown-up version of the young Ricardo Montalbán. His attire consisted of a tiny patch of underwear that looked like a black handkerchief and matching string. He had what appeared to be a permanent sneer stamped on his face and barely looked at me. Without uttering a word, he turned on his bare heel and proceeded down a dimly lit, drafty corridor half the length of a soccer field. Apparently I was supposed to follow.

The corridor felt oddly familiar, and then I recalled l'Ossuaire Municipal of Paris, where the bones of millions of nameless Parisians from previous centuries had been sorted and stacked beneath the streets in vile, unforgettable, cave-like tunnels that were now a macabre tourist attraction. My nearly naked guide was in an unexplained hurry, his bare feet practically skipping across the stone floor. Beads of sweat formed on his muscled back. "Making a Tarzan movie, I presume?" I said to his backside.

He didn't acknowledge me. Why was I the one to feel ridiculous? He was the one with the bare, hairy ass. At last he stopped at a door with no name or number displayed. He punched out a code on the computerized lock and led me inside, where he switched on a small reading lamp set on an end table, revealing that we were in what might have been a reception room. Everything was scrubbed and expensive. He closed the door and seated himself on a sofa next to the lamp, crossing his legs female fashion, one knee on top of the other. "You are a man of the world, are you not?" he asked me in his smug Spanish accent.

I dropped the clipboard and empty brown package at his feet. "Your attire, or lack of it, insults me," I said. "And you didn't ask me to sit down, which insults me again. Now you ask a strange question that's designed, I suppose, to keep me off-guard. This would be a good time for you to explain your bat-shit behavior, but to tell the truth, Tarzan, I'm not interested. Where's Borges?"

One eye narrowed and twitched just a moment. "You caught me at an inconvenient moment, yet I let you in. I don't have to apologize for my attire. I'm the one who belongs here. But let's not quarrel. My name is Jorge." He leaned forward to shake my hand. A test I couldn't possibly pass. If I shook it, he'd remain in control. If I didn't, I'd be ratcheting up the hostility, but to what purpose? I shook what turned out to be a sweaty palm. Two gaudy rings.

"I'm Lenny," I replied, still standing.

"Lenny, again I ask you. You are a man of the world, are you not?"

"What's that got to do with anything?" I asked him back, realizing even as the words left my mouth that this passive-aggressive response would only keep him in the driver's seat. He uncrossed his legs and immediately crossed them again, Sharon Stone style. Behind him was a closed door, and I tried to listen for any kind of sound, but I had only seventy percent hearing in one ear due to a bandit attack several centuries earlier in Florence. It's why the IDF wouldn't accept me for the infantry. They'd tried to make me a clerk.

"It's getting late, and I need to see Borges. Why don't you say what you have to say? Say it fast, and get me Borges."

"You are precisely as I expected," he said. "This pleases me."

"My truck is double-parked."

"Surely you have time to accept a gift," he said. His sneer transformed into a supercilious smile. "A gift of great value to a man of taste, a man of the world. Come, we invite you to share."

He rose, punched a code into the lock and opened the door behind him. I followed him into a totally dark room, and the door closed behind us. I sensed someone or something else breathing, but couldn't be sure.

"Lenny," he scolded me, "don't be nervous." His voice seemed to float from above or even below me.

"Ohhh!" A chilling wail, an anguished lament.

"Ruth!" I screamed into the darkness.

Something smashed my Adam's apple. Unbearable pain as a forearm squeezed my throat in a vice. I saw blackness inside the blackness and then what may have been a tumbleweed. I was inside it, the motion comforting, the feeling warm and eternal, like a mother's breast. But the speed picked up.

Now the tumbleweed's gone. Dizzy, scared, I'm in a bar, varnished, red wood all around me, and a crowd of drinkers. Above the bartender is a kayak carved from the same red wood. The place teems with señoritas. Gringos ply them with tequila. The bartender, a *chica* in hot pants, belts down her shot like a merchant seaman and slams her glass on the bar.

The place has that strained quality of manufactured gaiety, pretty girls licking the ears of fat, sweaty men. A saucy woman with streaked, ironed hair, straight and shiny, flashes me a look of disgust, then tosses her head like a filly. She shows off a cute butt in skintight jeans with gold lamé shoes and a wide, matching belt. I feel I know her. But where do old hookers go? Jesus, no, it's Ruth, and she's chewing gum, eyes half-closed, with Jorge's arm around her. His fingertips play with a nipple. But now he's a drunken priest, a conquistador in a grayish robe who stinks like the devil and there's no bar any-more, no kayak, just a dirt-floor bordello with rough-hewn tables and Indian slave girls who never smile no matter how much mescal they're forced to drink. It's clear that the Span-iards knock them about, trying to carve expressions in their stony faces. My father looks up, then recommences inspecting an evil-looking blade like a man reading a blueprint.

The Beast laughs, just as he did in Russia when he shipped an innocent boy to Siberia. I tear the head off somebody's shoulders and bring it down with all my strength on The Beast's skull. It cracks like an egg, but another Beast comes forward, unflappable, menacing. I crack his skull too. They push in from all sides, a crowd of Beasts, and I keep cracking them like Samson swinging the jawbone of an ass, but my arms are turning to lead. I hear a terrified voice, an icicle to the heart: "Who are you!" it screams. "Who are you!" I fear it's my own voice. I drop the skull and tighten my grip on a blade, ready to pull it across the priest's throat, except it may be Jorge's throat. "Not yet, not yet," hollers Ray Powell. Or is it my father? I'm so clumsy, so ill-informed. The Inquisitor of Toledo dines on goose and watches me with terrifying dispas-sion. "Ohhh!" Ruth wails.

"Who are you!" the voice cries once again.

But now, oh Jesus, I'm in jail. No more laughter, no bor-dello, no Beast or Ruth or conquistadores. Just me and my homicide. I must escape, but my legs are rubber, and this is no dream.

CHAPTER 18

LENNY

Ruth, just the other side of the dirty jail glass, looked like she'd just slogged through two back-to-back shifts bussing tables, but she remained remarkably striking, a work of art in simple skirt and blouse, no jewelry. Her hair was up. Stray, fine hairs played along the edges of her translucent ears. The smudged window and harsh fluorescent glare gave her an opaque quality, as though she were an image on a fuzzy TV screen and it was up to my imagination to fill in the blanks. Her voice was conveyed over crackling, long-neglected phone wires.

"Ben warned me you'd kill somebody. He begged me to call the police."

Of course jailers could be taping everything, but I didn't care. Men on either side conversed with women next to Ruth. Inmates and visitors alike had battled the same torpid, indifferent jail bureaucracy to get here and take a turn talking across a mucky window. It made you want to say important things, something that would make all the trouble worthwhile. But I had too much to tell her, too much and not enough.

"You know," I said, "this was always my worst nightmare, jail. But it's nothing, really. When the worst comes, it's nothing."

She said something about someone who might be called Jorge. It took a half-beat to absorb her words. So he was the one killed. The pompous pissant in the black thong. He needed killing anyway. "Where's my bracelet?"

"They must have taken it. They take everything."

They do. They take everything. "But you're not crying anymore, and that's good."

"Oh, Lenny." Her eyes moistened.

"I guess you're determined not to listen to me. But it's okay. I love you anyway."

That made her smile. "Let's face it. I love you too. What's your lawyer say?"

"He says we've got 'em right where we want 'em."

"Really."

"No. I'm lying to make you feel better."

I hazily recalled my attorney, but nothing about my arrest and very little of my first day in the Tombs. I remember waking up in a blue jumpsuit that smelled like its previous occupants. On Day Two they woke me very early for a trip to court, first sticking me in a holding cell with dozens of other men whose luck had run out. It was about three A.M., according to prisoner consensus in our clock-less environment. Shackled inside a van, I was transported around the corner to the Manhattan Criminal Courts Building, where it took them several hours to figure out I'd been deposited in the wrong courtroom. Somehow I got blamed. It was late afternoon when I was placed in another courtroom across the hall where, still chained, I was led to the proper seat.

I pleaded not guilty to a stack of charges that included first-degree murder, but only after the judge, a stocky African-American woman with a comedic flair, agreed with the D.A.'s office that I wasn't Leonard Hastings. "Since you have so far refused to identify yourself, I have no choice but to call you Mister Doe," the judge had said. "And incidentally, Mr. Doe, the bail is set at no bail. Even if we were to put aside the seriousness of the charges, which we won't, we couldn't consider putting you back on the street if we don't know who you are. *Capisce?*"

"*Mi resulta che atteggiamento completamente, signora giudice.*"

"What was that?"

"*Mi resulta che—*"

"What language was that?"

"The same one you spoke to me, madam judge. Italian."

"You speak Italian?"

"I get by."

The judge addressed the courtroom. "Anybody else here speak Italian? Come on, this is the Big Apple. *Some*body must speak Italian."

A middle-aged woman toward the rear raised her hand uncertainly.

"Would you stand up, please?"

The woman shook her head in resignation and stood up.

"What'd he say?"

"Something like, he understands completely."

"Ask him something in Italian."

"Ask him what?" asked the woman, half-confused, half-irritated.

"Anything. Ask him where he's from. No, wait. He heard that. Ask him something else."

"*I* don't know what to ask him."

The judge looked toward the ceiling, as though someone or something up there might deliver her from woman's inhumanity to woman.

"*Si prega di non avere problemi in te, signora,*" I told the woman.

"What was that?" asked the judge, excited.

"*Si prega di—*"

"Not you!" she shrieked. "You!" She lifted her chin toward the woman.

"He says I shouldn't get myself into trouble."

The judge nodded, deep in thought.

"He asked me nicely," the woman added. "Not like some people."

"Where'd you learn Italian?" the judge asked me.

"Can I sit down?" the Italian-speaking woman called out.

"Yes, thank you," said the judge, not taking her eyes off me. "Well?"

"Sorry, madam judge. I respectfully decline to answer."

The judge called the prosecutor to the bench for a hurried conference. My court-appointed attorney reluctantly joined them, but he appeared more interested in brushing dandruff off his shoulders. He'd introduced himself with a nod of his head minutes earlier and told me to plead not guilty no matter what.

I'm not sure why I toyed with the judge that way. For a long time I'd made a point of never using a language in a land where it didn't belong. It invited too many questions. But when you issue people filthy clothing, insult them, yell at them, feed them only occasional slop, and haul them around in chains to the wrong destinations, they get irritated.

Of course no one could place my accent, which I can't seem to extinguish entirely. I even speak Hebrew with an indeterminate accent. The police brought in an expert from a local college, but he couldn't pinpoint my origins either. Meanwhile, cops had already fingerprinted me three times, growing more irritated each time. "Where you from, dipshit?" was one of the nicer things they said. In the digital, twenty-first century world, they weren't used to drawing blanks.

"Sorry, I have to race to another courtroom," my lawyer told me. His office was in Queens, according to his business card, which I later threw away. I just wanted to get to Ruth. The rest was theater. On day three, when Ruth came to see me, it was encouraging to know that at least for those moments she wasn't with Borges.

"The bible says Isaac had children," she said. "He died just like I remembered, after a hundred and fourscore (telephone squawk), being old and full of days. He was buried by his sons, Jacob and Esau. Genesis 35:29."

"Ever wonder how Noah herded those centipedes into the ark? Plus cockroaches, gorillas, pythons? Ever try to determine the gender of a python? Must have been a real logistical nightmare, plus all the different dietary demands."

She briefly closed her eyes and shook her head in a quick no, signaling a switch of topics. "Lenny— Should I call you Lenny? Because whoever you (squawk), you're not Lenny . . . I guess you're a paranoid schizophrenic."

"Nobody's perfect."

"It's not funny."

"Then how come you're smiling?"

"Because now you're making *me* nuts too. I almost forgot—they tell me you speak Italian."

"Not enough to brag about. And just call me Lenny."

"*Ti amo,* Lenny."

"*Anche io,*" I said. Me too.

She was pleased to see my ear bandaged at last. The judge saw to that. A doctor with a droopy eye and pronounced nicotine stains on his fingers had drained it in the infirmary.

Ruth and I lapsed into a brief but sweet and comfortable silence until a guard came by and briefly addressed her. "Five minutes," Ruth told me, relaying the message as she looked my way with undisguised longing. If I couldn't find something to take my mind off it I'd have to hurl myself at the glass.

"Look, would you ask Borges to come see me?"

"He doesn't even know you, Lenny."

"Just ask him, okay? And I forgot to ask. How did I get arrested? I don't remember any of it."

"I don't know."

"But you were there."

She shook her head no again. "I don't— I'm a mess, Lenny. It's all a blank."

"Don't worry about it," I said. "Just remember, *ti amo.*"

"You don't know me. Not really."

"Be strong. I know he has power, but I'll get out of here and help you."

"I don't (squawk) you."

"What?"

"I don't deserve you."

The guard spoke again to Ruth, who nodded and hung up, her eyes on me, evaluating my relative sanity, wondering about her own too. Rather than obsess on all the harm I'd caused her, I tried to think of some way to reverse it.

After I was led away, when I played her words through my mind, I realized I should have asked her about this person who'd wanted her to call the cops. She must be close to him. Ben somebody.

RUTH

"Look, can you help me or not?"

A sovereign in his think tank universe, Borges sat in his soft leather, ergonomic chair, an abstract sculpture by Max Ernst taking up the corner to his left, and the breathtaking Manhattan skyline behind it on two sides of his corner office. He removed the slice of lemon from his glass of Perrier, smoothed his silky hair and said nothing, which from glib Borges was a resounding reply.

"Have you even spoken to anybody?" I asked him.

Without apology he took a call on his cell phone, listened awhile, said okay, and clicked the phone shut.

I still failed to understand the circumstances of Jorge's death and Lenny's arrest. The details weren't in the papers either. Yet they'd already convicted "Ruth Canby's Phantom Lover" for breaking into my "love nest" and murdering my "underling," "aide," "assistant," "subordinate," or, as Jorge was called in some news accounts, my "salaried lover." TV coverage was even more rabid. Coarse paparazzi hung around my building entrance poised to spring at anything, uniting my co-op neighbors into a sputtering, litigious lynch mob in pursuit of yours truly.

Meanwhile Borges, in all the accounts I'd seen, was quoted only in respect to his role as executive director of the Arthur Trianon Institute. He was never placed at the death scene, though I was fairly certain he'd been there. When I tried to remember the events of that night, I saw only hideous details of me and Jorge together. Then it would all go blank, and I'd be crushed by overwhelming regret and self-loathing. I appeared to be punishing myself for even *trying* to remember. It was like having an electrified door inside my mind. When I touched the knob, I could almost smell my flesh sizzle. Neither could I remember what I'd told the detectives. But whatever it was, they hadn't been back to see me.

"If you won't help," I said, "you could at least stop working against me."

"Ruth, you're not making sense."

"You told reporters you wouldn't rush to judgment because 'they' haven't had their day in court. Who's 'they'? You talk as though I'm a codefendant."

He picked up his glass of Perrier, studied it in the light, and set it down without drinking. "A figure of speech, I suppose, if I said it at all. I realize you're under terrible strain, but please, you don't actually believe what you read in the papers, do you?"

"I believe you always say exactly what you want to say precisely the way you want to say it, and you always remember what you said."

"Really, darling, get hold of yourself. I'm on *your* side. But try to understand. Everyone wants you crucified, and I'm just one imperfect man with my finger in the dike, if you'll excuse the mixed metaphor. I spend half my time defending you from the university and the other half trying to ward off your impossible neighbors in the co-op. They've jammed my voice mail with their wretched hollering, mostly reading me some morals clause. I barely have time to soothe our contributors. I haven't heard from Arthur Trianon yet, but when I do it won't be pleasant. Five minutes after we put his name on the stationery, an employee is found naked and strangled in our office. It's not the sort of name recognition he'd been aspiring to. Besides which, Jorge, you must recall, was the nephew of *another* important benefactor. I warned you about that."

"You warned me? What does that even mean?"

"Sorry, figure of speech."

"It was vague. You're vague only when there's a purpose to it, Borges. I know you. And *our* office? If I'm not mistaken, he was found in your suite at the office. Your private suite."

"Darling, you're right again. And of course I cherish the principle of academic freedom. But we're testing it here, Ruth. We're really testing it."

He'd deftly changed the subject from whether he'd cash in some chips to help Lenny, to whether I'd keep my job and my apartment.

"Forget all that crap, Borges. It doesn't interest me."

"Well, it sure as hell interests everyone else."

"Lenny, remember? What about Lenny?"

"I haven't forgotten, believe me. How could I with all this coverage? Look, would you please stop pacing and take a seat? Maybe we can tone down the level of hysteria inside this room at least. Please."

I seated myself at the edge of the four thousand-dollar Nicoletta armchair with chrome-plated swivel.

"What I'm told is— Well, let's just say the case has taken yet another bizarre twist," he said.

"Well?" I opened my palms and fluttered my fingers impatiently, nervously, despairingly.

"Of course they still don't know who he is, other than the fact that the person he claimed to be died two weeks after his birth in Chicago. They know he's fluent in Italian, and they've relayed his fingerprints to Italy and Switzerland, so far with no results. He still says he has no recollection of what occurred in this building, but there's plenty of physical evidence against him. Plus, of course, he'd followed a premeditated scheme to gain entrance. What's new is this. They now believe he looted a museum, or at the very least is a receiver of stolen property. But they can't figure out which museum, if you can believe that."

"I don't know what you're talking about. But he wants you to come see him."

"Me? Are you sure? What would he want with me? . . . Anyway, when they took him into custody, he was wearing a bronze armband that dates back to approximately 2,000 B.C., possibly even earlier. I imagine they'll be asking you about it. Presumably you saw him with his shirt off."

"I did, Borges. I did."

His face showed that my answer was too enthusiastic. "My, you're a sexy wench. Come here."

"No."

"Come here."

I no longer questioned why I obeyed Borges in these matters, but I knew he had the power to lower me to new depths of degradation. There were moments when I felt my own strength, but in the end he always reduced me to the dirt of my origins.

There's something called the imposter syndrome. When people advance quickly, they can create a gap between how others see them and how they see themselves. They believe they're protecting the secret of terrible inadequacies and are in constant fear they'll be unmasked. It's quite common among stars in the sports and entertainment worlds. When they suddenly start earning millions, they feel unworthy and come apart, sometimes very quickly, sometimes over a period of years, like Billy Blankenship.

The fact that Michel Houellebecq and I had both been abandoned as children and gone on to succeed in similar occupations should have made us a dynamic duo, but it didn't work that way. Victims don't always bond well because what they share is guilt and shame. Yad Vashem and similar memorials are only partially successful attempts to assign humiliation to perpetrators rather than survivors.

I fell to my knees and crept on all fours to Borges. "It's nothing to cry about, darling." He traced a thumb down my cheek and grinned as though pleased with an obedient spaniel. I touched his hand lightly and grinned. I caressed his wrist with my fingers, and sank my teeth into a finger, grinding and ripping into the bone.

"Eeeeyahhh!" Unable to shake me loose, he slapped me away with the back of his other hand. I exploded into laughter as he tore off his screwball headband and pressed it over the wound. I was delirious with ecstasy and hate. But when I saw his eyes, I had to look away.

CHAPTER 19

RUTH

It wasn't until later, going home in the taxi, that I reflected on the impossible coincidence that neither I nor Lenny could recall whatever had transpired in Borges's suite. My memory of that night was in a hole so black that I couldn't even sort out simple bits of information disgorged by the news media.

"Odd things happen around Borges," said Ben the next morning. "I can't explain them either, but I'm on your side now." I was so glad to see him that I didn't focus on the puzzle that had to lurk behind his words.

Ben had quit his job on the coast, taken a night flight to Newark and a cab straight to me. He looked at me uncertainly across my kitchen table and took another sip of instant coffee. When Ben drinks your instant coffee, you know he must be very fond of you.

"You'll never guess what they told me, when I finally just bugged out." He was obviously pleased with himself.

"They didn't," I said, playing along with his game.

"Not in so many words, but the gist of it? Absolutely. You'll—"

"—never work in this town again." We yelled it out together. And . . . I laughed—and laughed some more because I was so delighted to be laughing again. As for Ben, he nearly spritzed coffee out his nose.

"But Ben, seriously, wasn't that your dream? A Hollywood—" Before I could utter the word "feature," I started laughing again. When your friend throws away something precious, I guess all you can do is laugh.

"I just never felt it, you know? Never felt easy or comfortable. They gave me nothing to work with, and my life was just a bad dream. No, two dreams. First the one where you show up somewhere naked and confused and everyone's staring at you. And there were these endless, you know, discussions."

"In the dream?"

"No, for real. I mean, I love endless discussions as much as the next person, but nothing was ever decided; and meanwhile I've got all these passive-aggressive crazies fidgeting outside the door and I'm sucking down ginkgo biloba with Twinkies and caffeine and it was— The other dream, it was the college dream, the one where you forgot there was a final—or you forgot about the whole course even and missed every class— but somehow you show up and everybody else is halfway through the test already. I must have lived that dream every minute I was out there."

"It's my fault, isn't it?"

"Don't ever repeat this, Ruth. Swear it."

"Repeat what?"

"Just swear."

"I swear already."

"I was just too old to make the change. I need to be in my own little pond. I know that now, but I'd sold my chubby ass for twenty pieces of silver, and I couldn't get out of it, and suddenly I realized, Ben, you *can* get out of it. Find the best hundred and ten minutes you can and get the hell out."

"Why a hundred and ten?"

"Because anything important runs over ninety, but this monstrosity couldn't hold up for seventy-five, so I chose a number halfway between total surrender and the pretense of significant filmmaking."

"Look me in the eye and tell me I had nothing to do with your coming back."

"Well, of course you were all over the Internet and every-thing, and sure, I was dying to get at all the inside dope other gossipmongers can only guess at. So come on, sweetie, dish out the dirt. Make it snappy and tacky. Don't you just *love* tabloid news?" I tapped him with a bunny punch to the chest, making him beam. "I mean what's so terrible? You realize how many people out there would give anything to be caught in a love nest? Just what *is* a love nest anyway? They never make it clear. Are they lined with twigs or what?"

"Oh shut up. It isn't funny."

"Sure it is."

"I'm so glad you're back."

He took my hand and kissed it with perfect gallantry.

I still couldn't bear to tell him the true nature of my relationship with Borges, or at least as much as I understood about it. When I gingerly mentioned Lenny's Isaac fantasy he barely quizzed me about it. I didn't think it odd at the time. I was also aware that all the paranoid pieces of Lenny's hallucination were holding up, right down to the curious arm bracelet. Not that I believed he was a four thousand-year-old biblical character, but certain forms of madness could be like the dreams that Jung concluded are a door to both the unconscious *and* the supernatural. I loved the whole of Lenny, and if a part of him was oracular or even crazy, I decided I'd just have to love that part too.

"Look, you have to at least tell me about the shiner, okay?"

"It's not really a black eye. Or did it get worse?"

"Trust me. If you go out there, do it in dark glasses."

"Shit." I ran into my bedroom and took another look.

"Just needs a little makeup," I told Ben without conviction. But measured against the recent pattern of my life, the purple flesh around my eye was small potatoes. Ben was digging into a yogurt he'd scavenged from the refrigerator. His comfort level in my apartment perked me up a little. When your life turns into a constant stream of turmoil and disaster, you need to take pleasure in anything remotely encouraging.

"The black eye isn't his fault," I explained. "He was just trying to get away."

"Back up. Wasn't whose fault?"

"Borges's."

"What was he trying to get away from?"

"Me. I'd just bitten him."

Ben's eyes grew wide. His complexion grayed. What was this? I took his hand and squeezed.

"You okay?"

"No. I'm not particularly okay," he said, "but tell me everything."

I didn't, but I told him enough. "He'd been hinting he could help Lenny somehow, but he wouldn't do it, and I just despised him anyway, and all of a sudden it just, I don't know, erupted. I—" I shook my head, unable to even hint at my vile, uncontrollable self, much less the inexplicably degenerate details of my relationship with Borges. I'm sure Ben guessed them anyway.

"You're so brave," he said. There was wonder in his voice but also a kind of mourning for something lost, and his eyes were tearing. "But what were you thinking?"

I handed him a tissue. "About Lenny, I think. It gave me strength."

"He's such a devious, devious . . . man, Borges, and I pushed you into his arms."

"I make my own decisions, Ben. Don't be silly, okay? I should have listened to you and called the cops. But why— How come neither of us can remember what happened that night? Not me *or* Lenny? I can't even *try* to remember. It makes me physically ill."

Ben dabbed at his eyes. I reached out and held on to his shoulder. The phone rang. I let the machine answer it. The voice at the other end said, "Darling, if you're there, pick up."

Borges. My insides quivered. Ben grabbed the phone and stared at it as though he held a dead rat. Finally he put it to his ear. "Don't—" His voice shook. "Don't call here."

"Ben? Is that you?" Borges's voice was still coming through the answering machine speaker.

"Yes."

"What in God's name are you doing in New York? Have you lost your mind?"

"Ruth needs time alone."

"Then what are you doing over there?"

"I— Well, I—"

"Put her on the phone."

I hit the button that took the call off the speaker and gently took the receiver from Ben. He'd aged ten years in two minutes, as though some sinister auditing procedure had reversed the results of all the surgeries and chemicals.

"Darling, we need to speak," Borges said.

Why did I take the phone from Ben? We couldn't help each other. Not really. I was terrified and alone.

"I have information regarding your Lenny." I couldn't take my eyes off Ben. "I need to speak with you here."

I was afraid to go, afraid to disobey. "Did you hear me?"

"That would be . . . awkward," I stammered.

"Not at all. You're under great strain. I know that. Last night never happened. Don't speak of it."

"What's he saying?" whispered Ben. He was shrinking. Not physically. His presence was shrinking. If I didn't acknowledge it, maybe it would stop.

"I'll send a car for you."

"What's he want?" asked Ben, not quite whispering now.

"Don't tell me Ben got fired," Borges said.

"He quit," I said.

Ben's face was turned toward the window. "Don't," he said. Frantic. Almost shouting. "Please don't!" He sank hard to both knees, clutching his chest, his face, his chest again, emitting simultaneous dread and terror. It poured out of him like smoke. I knelt and took him in my arms. His face was blue. I scrambled for the phone and shouted.

"Don't Borges! Don't! I'm coming, I'll come!"

LENNY

The Tombs, impossibly crowded and cruel, pulsates with a generic fury, waiting always for an excuse to pop. For their own safety, guards pretend the banned inmate radios that are everywhere don't exist. Rap dominates and practically rules in the form of a crazy cacophony of competing stations that raises the level of atmospheric madness. But on my third night, from somewhere down the tier, I heard an amplified voice of another kind—a voice that somehow tore through the noise and bluster, the clanking and shouting and out-loud anguish and spite. The song was an anthem to another kind of misery, an anguish devoid of fury or blame.

> *When a man loves a woman*
> *Can't keep his mind on nothing else*
> *He'll trade the world*
> *For the good thing he's found . . .*

The lyrics by themselves could be seen as hopeful, but the singer (I found out later his name was Percy Sledge) let you know otherwise, that woeful dues must be paid and paid again before the wretched outcome that must come. He'd stripped his soul down to its shredded core, and the power of his song was still capable of moving souls suffering in the hell of The Tombs fifty years after he'd made the recording. The backup singers, mouthing no words, hummed like gospel instruments, turning his passionate declaration into an anthem.

> *He'd give up all his comfort*
> *Sleep out in the rain*
> *If she said that's the way it ought to be . . .*

I ached with each note, for Ruth, for me, for lost love and lovers, for Sledge's exquisite lament and for all the slaves I'd known over time because the song and the singer were spawned from slavery. Nothing else could create its pained, plaintive splendor.

The detectives who'd just interrogated me again assumed a dark core to all that's human—that everyone lies about everything—every merchant a swindler, every woman a cheat, every child a sneak. Percy Sledge reminded me that though the cosmos may be exasperating and indifferent, there are oases of sweet sincerity.

Once I watched a woman weep as she stood before a canvas in a Brussels gallery. More than a century ago. The painting depicted gaslight reflected in a river, stars overhead, two lovers strolling in the foreground. But within that routine structure the artist, with his brushstrokes and colors, his shapes and subtle choices, had opened a door to all the grace of the universe. He'd made the light dance for anyone who cared to look.

The tearful woman had brown hair, arched brows, and eyes that haunt me still. Behind the trouble in them were endless possibilities. She was accompanied by a smartly dressed man, who, embarrassed by her tears, rushed her toward the door. As she passed we looked deeply into each other, afraid to act on what we both recognized, that the barest hesitation, a word, a hint of any kind would have sparked the flame. Van Gogh had painted fast, as he painted everything, because his mind saw everything at once. Mine failed to work as quickly and now the woman is dust. Letting her go was a sin.

In all the time I'd had on Earth, only there in the Tombs did I come to understand how grievously the grudge I'd carried for centuries had infected me, because the truth is I've committed far worse sins than my father. A person can't live in this world and do otherwise. If I could ask him one favor, I'd ask him to forgive me.

RUTH

Borges and I were sipping Manhattans in his office. Side by side, we leaned against the edge of his expansive desk and looked out at the New York night. His finger was heavily bandaged and covered with gauze that wrapped around his wrist, encompassing much of his hand. I'd removed my dark glasses to show the blue and green damage around my eye, but it failed to embarrass Borges, who was always content, always in control. We both waited to turn the conversation down a tributary we'd never taken before, one I knew he wouldn't enter until he was ready.

In the meantime he said he'd checked, and according to his source the district attorney's case against Lenny was much weaker than the media portrayed it. "Of course he also has that assault case in San Diego pending, but I know a trial attorney out there who's a courtroom magician, and he owes me a favor."

I was also concerned about Ben, even though he'd snapped back after that awful half-minute of pain or paralysis or whatever it was. Just to be sure, I dropped him off at an urgent care facility before taking the cab on to Rockefeller Center.

"Who are you, Borges? Who are you, really?"

"I am who I say I am, Ruth. I never lie to you. You should know that by now."

"You come close to telling me, but when I ask you to explain you act like I'm out of my mind."

"I asked you here because I'm offering you a new employment contract, darling. It's a very special contract, and I assure you I wouldn't offer it to someone I thought was out of her mind, or at least any more out of her mind than your average English lit professor."

"I'm not here about a new contract. I'm here to help Lenny. I'm here so you won't harm Ben."

He shook his head with a smile, signaling amusement at my naïveté. "You didn't need us for your book, you know. Or your next one either. You chose to believe fools who'd closed you up in their crumbling little mausoleum. There was no lock on the door, but you wouldn't leave on your own. That's part of being an orphan, I suppose. Not knowing who to trust, particularly when you need to trust yourself."

By ignoring my awful accusation, by paying no heed to the inexplicable events swirling around us, he was confirming something. I was breathing much too hard now. The more I tried to stop, the worse it got. I guzzled the rest of my drink and asked him again, "Who are you?"

"It gets tedious when you repeat the same question. Have some sympathy." He poured me another Manhattan from the pitcher.

"That's what you told Billy Blankenship, remember? The night we met. Have some sympathy, you said. You seemed to be joking, but then he died. And now—" Something was different about Borges. Nothing physically, nothing in his manner either, at least nothing I could pin down. Meanwhile I felt a surge of dread unlike any I'd ever experienced. And weakness. I shut my eyes. "I'm in Hell." I hadn't meant to say it aloud.

"No, you're not, actually. But I'd like you to see something, if you don't mind. Look at me. And don't be nervous. No one will hurt you."

I turned my head and saw the same amused, brown eyes framed by the sharp features of a smug, conceited man. But then I felt a tremor somewhere, a displacement in time and space. The earth twirled around the sun at real speed, hurtling through eternity as always, but now I was aware of it. If I looked away from him I'd be swept into the blackness, and as my eyes remained fastened to his I saw vapors rising from the ground, rivers slicing canyons into the earth and creatures that galloped across the horizon, changing form before my eyes. Life and death were one. There was no beginning, just the aching vastness of endless space and time and the fury of effortless beauty. Dawn and dusk mingled and light had no source. It just was. I trembled for the agonizing sweetness and terror of it all. I saw Lenny splayed upon a great rock, gazing into unbearable truth. A resolute figure raised an arm above him. I saw a little girl in a blue dress and shiny black shoes. A merry-go-round. My mother smiled one last time. I smelled her lipstick and was at home inside her blue-green eyes, remembered her broad forehead, her strong arms around me. "Mommy," I said. *Oh, now I see, now I see.* And there was Borges again, trying to tell me something.

"Follow me." He started for the door and looked back. "You can do it. Just take one step, then another."

He led me into the chilly, deserted corridor. A baleful breeze swirled around my ankles as I marched behind him like a condemned prisoner. Absolute quiet. We turned some corners and stopped finally at an unmarked door that looked like all the others. Opening it, he led me down a dank, barely lighted stairway. Descending old wooden steps, I smelled rotting meat. Faint sounds of whimpering. When we reached bottom I felt my way along the wall, following Borges as he turned a corner into another room. It held about twenty cubicles, each with a computer monitor. Their dim screens were the only source of light. Seated at them were barely human-looking wretches, their faces contorted in various expressions of anxiety, concern, and desperation. I heard steady whimpering now, an occasional cough. Each specter was attached to the floor by one leg iron. The meat smell was overpowering.

"The scholars," I heard myself whisper. I don't know how long I stood there.

"Come," Borges said evenly, leading me out. The whimpers intensified, turning into harder cries of grief like the bleating of doomed sheep, as though our visit had generated a smidgeon of possibility that was now degenerating into renewed hopelessness and abandonment. Ignoring their cries, Borges turned his head and flashed a terrifying smile. Sobbing, I followed him back to his office.

"Take a seat," he told me. Consumed by fear and waves of nonspecific grief, I did as I was told. He stood beside the Max Ernst sculpture against the window. A helicopter moved across the sky. He handed me my glass. I drained half and set it down, wondering what I'd done, what awful choice I'd made to bring me here, to this place, and I was sorry for everything I'd done to deserve it. Only my curiosity, which had always been mother and father to me, helped me endure.

"Is there some reason for keeping them like that? Or is it just madness?" He looked at me with a blank expression I'd seen on him many times before. Only now did I begin to understand it. "Is . . . one of those leg irons waiting for me?"

This amused him. "I take it you prefer your old contract then."

"Do I have a choice?"

"Of course. But I need to know your preference."

"No . . . contract at all then."

"You want to resign. You want neither the old contract nor the new one."

"Yes."

"Done." Reading my disbelief, he added, "How many times do I have to tell you that I never lie to you?"

"There's a catch, Borges. There's a catch." I tried so hard not to whine. "Please stop toying with me. Please. Have pity."

"There's no catch. You can walk away, from me, the Arthur Trianon Institute, all of it. Go back to L.A. if you like. You're a serious author now. You can live anywhere you like."

"But I can't write anymore. I—"

"I think you'd find yourself unblocked."

"And . . . I never have to see you again?"

"That's an ugly way to put it. Try to curb your hostility. It's unbecoming. Especially in such a glorious creature."

"Why did you show them to me then? The ones . . . below . . . if you're letting me go?"

"It's not important. You resigned, remember?"

"But what about Ben? And Lenny?"

"This is not a negotiation. Besides, Ben's already gone."

"No." I grasped my hair with both hands. "No, no, no."

"You know? That's always amazed me. People are genuinely surprised when someone dies."

My mind stumbled, unable to integrate this moment with all that I'd known before. I'm not sure what happened next, but I remember eventually sinking to both knees to beg for Ben's life.

"But he's gone, Ruth. There was a call from the clinic. He was older than he looked, you know, and his heart and lungs shut down. He had too many obligations to meet. It was all too much for him, and they just couldn't save him. I'm sorry. Truly I am."

"No you're not, you're not," I wailed as though his lack of remorse were more significant than the death itself. The painful timbre of my voice frightened me.

Ben had shared his secret in the back of our taxi. "Oh Ruth, please don't look at me." He emitted a groan of chilling anguish, then buried his face, so much older than it had been, on my shoulder. I held his head, running my fingers lightly through his hair. Transplanted little tufts came away in my hands. "Borges sent me after you. From the beginning. He knew you'd be kind to an old queer and his screwed-up son. Can you forgive me? Because everything we had, it felt real to me. I wanted . . . I want it all to be real."

"It's real, Ben. If we both want it to be, then it's real."

He looked up and smiled through his tears. When I kissed him goodbye in the waiting room of the clinic, he was already joking with the receptionist but in an older voice. I desperately wanted to stay with him but was afraid what Borges might do if I made him wait. Now Ben was gone anyway—after confirming my wildest paranoid guesses, the kind you don't even want to acknowledge to yourself. But Lenny—of course, Lenny was alive. He must be. I pleaded with Borges for his freedom. "Lenny is— He's Isaac, isn't he? What happens to him when I—"

"Quit?"

I nodded slowly.

"Look, you want my advice?"

I picked up my glass but couldn't drink.

"Walk away, Ruth."

"What do I have to do to save Ben and Lenny?"

"I told you, Ben's gone. As for Lenny— You want to, as you say, save Lenny?"

"Yes."

"No, I can't let you."

"Please, what do I have to do?"

"It's crazy."

"What?"

"You'd have to sign the new contract."

"All right, let me see it."

"Oh, there's no time for that. You just have to trust me. Also, if you stay with us—"

"I'd be down . . . with the others?"

"I never said that."

"Where then?"

"Ruth, dear, those are your *colleagues* down there. Aren't you concerned for them? Don't you want to save them too?"

"I— I asked you before. Is there a reason you keep them like that? Or is it just madness?"

"So it's just about you and Lenny. You don't need to save everybody." He was terribly amused.

"That's not a real choice, is it?"

He shook his head. I couldn't bear his eyes, but I couldn't look away.

"What's in the contract? How long is it?"

"Stay on now and you'd become family, Ruth. *Family*. You'd like that, wouldn't you? An orphan no more. But I must have your loyalty. Do you understand? I'm sorry if it sounds peculiar. But if you stay with us I'd have to have it. You must *pledge* your loyalty."

"Okay." The word came out in a guttural voice I didn't recognize.

"I want you to be sure, Ruth, because this is irrevocable, do you understand? But you needn't worry. You know I adore you. And our arrangement so far hasn't been so awful, has it?" His fingers brushed a few stray hairs off my face. I closed my eyes as they teared with shame and ecstasy.

Chapter 20

Lenny

Ruth sat frightened in the dirt, surrounded by some unspecified malevolence. The scene was familiar to me, yet hazy, a recurring agony in a recurring vision that could be memory or perhaps a window into the present—or future. Impossible to sort out. A crowd of idle spectators watched her as one might watch a fish in a tank. She lit up when she spotted me, but my legs were numb, I was mute. She stared in disbelief and mouthed words I couldn't hear.

After breakfast, I found The Beast seated at a surprisingly clean table inside a stark room we had to ourselves. He didn't have to converse through a dirty window over a junk phone like everyone else. "Please allow me to introduce myself," he said. "I'm Anton Borges." He wore a necklace and bracelet of seashells and a red kerchief headband. Not what I expected, but surprise had always been one of his tools. I seated myself across from him. *We've spoken before.* But I couldn't get the words out. I took a deep breath. "You didn't have to harm Ruth to get to me," I half-squeaked.

He inspected me as though I were an odd, caged creature. Neither of us made a move to shake hands. One of his fingers was elaborately bandaged. So was my ear. Neither of us asked about or expressed concern for the other. The jail doctor who'd drained my ear had instructed me to drop in again so he could check my progress. As though I could grab a cab from my cell.

"I understand completely why your recent experiences might leave you confused," The Beast said, "but I wouldn't dream of harming Ruth. In any case, you're the one in jail. Let's talk about you. You appear to be in a bad spot."

"What do you suggest? Prayer?" Words came easier now.

His lips formed a sardonic smile. "Jail seems like an apt place for it."

I'd waited a long time for this moment. But reaching it didn't feel like victory. Nothing good would come from this meeting. I pressed him anyway. "Would anyone be listening?" I said.

"Think of all those heartfelt pleas for the Giants to cover the spread against New England. It would be an awful waste of everyone's time if no one ever listened."

At that very moment, innocents sprinkled around the globe lived in a closed cycle of pain, hunger, disease, and the certainty of worse days to come. Lunatics raped and humiliated them, cut and burned, cheated and enslaved them. And they probably all prayed, victims and lunatics alike. Ruth might be praying right now.

"I suppose prayer isn't always answered with exactitude," said The Beast. Did he read my thoughts? "But it makes people *feel* better, don't you think? There must have been a time when you prayed."

"I heard no answers."

"You expected God to speak to you? That's a rather narcissistic view, wouldn't you say?"

"He spoke to my father."

"You're sure of that?"

"Someone did. Something . . . did." I decided that whatever I said to The Beast wouldn't matter. Neither cleverness nor reason was a factor. Nor even luck. He already knew what he was going to do, but he enjoyed tantalizing me with the idea that I might influence what secrets he might share or what he might do. And he was right. I kept trying. What else could I do? "Who are you?"

"I imagine you've thought about it, haven't you? Guess, why don't you?"

"A messenger," I said. "From where I don't know. Maybe God, maybe the devil."

My answer amused him—as a flying monkey might amuse him. "I'm terribly flattered. God or the devil. I see. That's quite a range though, isn't it?"

"Is it?"

"What do you mean?"

I could barely get the next words out. "Maybe there's no difference," I said.

"So you've considered that. Does it frighten you?"

"I suppose you . . . could also be the anti-Christ."

"You don't seem to have a very high opinion of me, do you? I suggest you just consider me a friend of Ruth. I'm here as a favor to her. But I expect you don't believe that. Well, anyway, it's very kind of you not to say it. And you do raise some interesting theological questions. Maybe you'll just have to die to find the answers."

"Would that work?"

"It's a common assumption, isn't it? Death clears it all up? Even the most egregious simpleton will know everything at last?"

"You're the one who spoke to my father, aren't you? Did *he* know who you were?"

Now there was delight in his eyes. He was delighted not to answer. Delighted that I would die in a state of ignorance, like everyone else. Everyone except suicide bombers. They seemed quite sure of themselves. "You still don't understand, do you?"

"Maybe it's my failure to understand that kept me going."

He shook his head. "Fear," he said. "Fear kept you going. The same fear that drives all the others, the same fear that made you run from me."

It was then, as I looked across the table at The Beast and his disdain, that I envisioned for the first time how the world would proceed without me. There was no hesitation in its step, no sign of the tiny space I'd once filled. In the fullness of time the memory of who I'd really been would be lost like the memory of all the disremembered souls in all the unmarked graves of time, like the memory of all the fools who, as Epicurus pointed out, were always getting ready to live.

I'd often mourned for people even while they lived. Only rarely did they understand how very close they were to their last breath. But I was the most lamentable of all. I'd *tried* to live in the now, to be conscious of *this moment* and revel in it, to learn at least that much. But the years had washed over me like waves, one after another. I never managed to sort them out or slow them down. Making only frivolous use of eternal youth and limitless experience, I'd accomplished no more than your average bug. The tale of Isaac would be told again and again, but it missed the essence of who I'd been and the lessons of my failure. Nor would it describe, as Shelley's monster lamented, how the breezes had once caressed my cheeks.

"You know," said The Beast, "Abraham gloried in being a patriarch. You, on the other hand, seek no recognition, no servants or followers. Let's just say for the purpose of this conversation that you are who you claim to be. Clearly you could have made yourself a wealthy man over time. But you were better than that. You're a good sort, Yitzhak. I'm fond of you." I searched his smile, and was startled to find it no longer sardonic but genuine. I wiped tears with my shirt. I don't think I'd cried in decades. Now I seemed to be crying every day or so.

"It's been so long," I explained, "since someone called me by my name." I was named for laughter because when God told my father I was coming, my elderly mother laughed at the preposterous promise.

"You've been in worse fixes, you know. You can still have a fine future. A lasting future."

"And Ruth?"

"Yes, Ruth. As we've both noticed, she's a terribly attractive, brilliant, one might say perfect woman. I'd like her to stay on with us at the institute. And I want you to agree."

"I don't understand. Agree to what?"

"We're her perfect instrument, Yitzhak. Just let her achieve her dream. And you and your remarkable journey will go on."

"But why am I on this journey?" A foolish waste of breath, I knew even as the words left my mouth. When he didn't answer, I asked him, "What if I don't agree? About Ruth staying on?"

"You know, if you were to obtain the right legal team these cases against you would most likely never go to trial." He named a lawyer friend who I happened to know handled much of Ray Powell's endless litigations. The lawyer was famous for once collecting a hefty judgment for a man who fell out of a hammock while screwing his girlfriend. "Just say the word and I expect you'll be out on your own recognizance in a day or two. The cases here and back in California can fall apart naturally, as so often occurs in these matters. I rather doubt your public defender would achieve the same result. Shall I make the call then?"

It was terribly seductive, the thought of going on after all. I could make that new start in Montreal and try again to prevent the tedium of everyday life from stealing the sensation of each miraculous moment.

"But Ruth won't be happy with you, will she?"

"Look around," he said. "Who's happy?"

"Let her go. And let me die."

"You think it's that simple, do you? You know, Yitzhak, I've thought about you from time to time. Long before this. Does that surprise you?"

Yes, it did. Even after learning that The Beast was out there, it hadn't changed my suspicion that I was a forgotten soul, perhaps blessed, but surely abandoned. He paused to stare deep into my eyes. His own were alarmingly composed, not derisive anymore, nor amused. I was staring now into blank pits, horrifying and deep as time. "I don't," he said, "have to bargain with you. I do as I please."

"Then why ask my permission?"

"Your father was prepared to sacrifice you for the greater good. You could be equally gracious."

"You mean I should sacrifice Ruth. But why does anyone have to sacrifice anyone else? Why must we be continually tested? What's it all for? You only want me to decide so I'll regret my decision later."

"Listen to what I'm saying. If you want out of here, to be free, completely free, just say so."

"Is that my purpose? To stay out of hell? Forget it. I'll take her place."

"What?"

"If my death's not enough for you, then I'll go wherever you like."

"You'll sign on at the institute?"

"Yes."

"You're no scholar, Yitzhak."

"Does it really matter?"

"It might to you. You'd have to fill Jorge's position."

"What did Jorge do besides run around with a hairy ass?"

"He did what he was told."

"How long was he with you?"

He burst into laughter, and it was a repugnant sound. Laughing not just at me or Ruth, but at the human condition. When it died down, he said, "You're already impatient to leave. But you should have learned patience by now, Yitzhak. Let's just say Jorge worked for me for quite some time. He learned to enjoy it eventually. You on the other hand—I understand why you might want to help Ruth. It's commendable, but it would be a mistake, Yitzhak, if you don't walk away."

"I'll take the job. But you let her go. No tricks."

"Don't speak to me like that."

I was swept by a terrible fear. I tried to fight it but had to bow my head from the force of it—and the pain and sorrow that now engulfed me. Was this my eternity? "May I see her? May I say goodbye to Ruth?"

He took a deep breath, and when he exhaled, some of the anger seemed to go out of him. I could breathe again. "A clever move, Yitzhak, asking my permission. It shows respect. Even if it's not sincere. It's not necessary to be sincere at first." He extended his uninjured right hand, possibly for a kiss? I wondered, not for the first time, what might follow if I were to leap at his throat and squeeze. He read my mind, of course, and it amused him. I was his flying monkey again. I shook his hand. It was warmer than I'd expected. "I'll send for you," he said, "when it's time." What did that mean to him? It could be ten thousand years. But I didn't think so.

They let me out the next morning on my own recognizance. They even returned my bracelet.

RUTH

Something told me Borges would let us see each other before the end, however it came. So I wasn't surprised to pick up the phone and hear Lenny's voice. "I'll meet you there," I told him. I no longer felt completely comfortable in my apartment, which, like so much of what I'd believed to be mine, came to me through Borges. Lenny's hotel was just off Riverside Drive, only a few blocks away. I wanted to make myself beautiful, but I couldn't bear the delay. Defeated by this simple conundrum, I sank into a chair and tried to calm myself. I'm not sure how much time passed before I threw on a jacket and flew past the young African man at the desk.

Gusts of wind blew daggers of freezing drizzle in the faces of pedestrians who suffered in silence as cabbies inched along the clogged streets honking at everything that displeased them. Bicycle messengers dodged chunks of gray ice and nannies pushing strollers. Sirens in the distance signaled someone else's troubles. Listen closely and you could hear the sound of souls unraveling. Were someone to sink to the pavement shrieking uncontrollably, I could easily imagine the others, neither pleased nor displeased, scooting around the casualty without looking back.

I speeded up along the slick sidewalks with the growing fear of another Borges trick, that something awful would happen before I reached Lenny. I swept through pedestrian spaces like a race car driver, becoming a target for everyone's animus. "Hey, babe, what the fuck." "Watch it!" Finally reaching an open stretch, I broke into a flat-out run, fearful, hopeful, crying, giggling. I mustn't break down, had to get there.

Lenny waited outside the entrance, looking just as frantic as I felt. "Oh Lenny, I saw my mother. I saw her."

LENNY

We folded each into the other, mingling tears and kisses in the cold rain. Finally I pulled her inside, past the kindly matron at the desk. The neighborhood was flush, the lobby neat and clean, but when the elevator doors opened you discovered the hotel was a masked, grimy dump of deferred maintenance, everything exhausted, chipped, faded, and disintegrating. Guests scurried in and out like furtive mice.

I mumbled excuses as I struggled with the key, and Ruth began to laugh through her lingering tears. Finally, when I pushed the door open across the ratty rug, she poked her head inside. "This looks like John Gotti's cell, only smaller," she said.

"We can find another then," I said, but followed her inside.

"I was just kidding. It's perfect, actually. Besides, I don't think we have much time."

How much did she know? "Everything's going to be fine," I said.

The spongy double bed took up most of the room. It was adorned by a bedspread not altogether clean. We stood on opposite sides, each waiting for the other like adolescents looking for clues. The awkwardness might have been funny under other circumstances because the bed was the only place to sit down, and there was barely space to stand. Suddenly I felt like the ancient man I was, afraid I'd disgust her.

"You're right," she said. "Everything's just fine. But you are Isaac, aren't you? You're not crazy at all. Can you forgive me?"

"I'm the one who needs forgiveness. What happened to your eye?"

"I bit Borges. It was funny. I'll explain later. Tell me about your life. Tell me everything. How on earth did you wind up in L.A.?"

She bit him! That explained his bandage. Why couldn't I summon such courage?

"Tell me . . . about you," she said.

"I'm just . . . not used to talking about it. I try to learn from the past, but I don't, at least not as much as I should. . . . I—"

"The only thing we learn from history is that we learn nothing from history. Hegel."

"Stop showing off," I said. Why did I say that?

"Why am I so nervous?" The question burst out of her as though she'd been holding it in. It might have come from me. She seated herself on the bed. "You were telling me about yourself."

"I don't know where to begin."

"Why not start at the beginning? Your first memories."

I sat down next to her. We held hands and gazed at the blank TV screen.

"I guess maybe we *should* talk," I said.

"Just things you've seen, people you've known. How are they different now? Or aren't they?"

"It feels so strange, talking about it. I just—"

"So you want to talk, but you don't want to talk about it?"

"Shut up."

"You shut up."

"We're lousy at this talking thing. Whose idea was it anyway?"

"Wasn't mine," she said, unbuttoning her blouse.

It had been too long, and we went too quickly, though there's something to be said for that too. Next thing I knew she was sticking her head out of the bathroom. "The only towel in here is wet."

"Sorry."

"This thing is barely a dish towel."

"It's what you get for a hundred a night in Manhattan. Besides, you said this place is perfect."

"I lied so I could have my way with you." She came out wearing my shirt.

"Don't wear that," I said. "I haven't washed it from jail."

"Okay." She threw it off.

"Damn, you're beautiful. You even move like you're beautiful. Like a dream."

"You too." She slid under the covers with me and placed a hand on my chest. "What did you do with your ankle thing? When you took a shower?" My jailers had fitted me with a tracking device.

"Nothing."

"You got it wet? Wasn't that against the rules?" She snuggled closer.

"Who are you gonna tell?" I hugged her tight. I had an altered relationship with death, and now I was very much aware that it has a sweet side, a singular, melancholy beauty in its shadow of outrageous finality. Without the certainty of death, you'd be cheated. I thought of the Samaritan girl whose mother told her so long ago that life is suffering. She didn't know the half of it.

RUTH

My future was a leap into a low flame. So why think about it? It would only lead to premature suffering. I decided there were no consequences. There was no end, no beginning, just a stream of moments that must be grasped, confronted, and embraced before they were lost.

I'd had students who, by their teenage years, were already too cool and world-weary to care what lay beyond the next hill. I understood now the glow of Lenny's presence. He'd spent centuries absorbing what was and wasn't worthwhile and decent. Despite all the horrors he must have seen, the disappointments he no doubt experienced, he remained an exquisite, deceptively simple being, curious and devoid of cynicism. And there I was, trying to dissect his allure, to run it through a logarithm. I'm such a jerk sometimes.

He described pieces of his life to me, beginning with his mother and father, though he wasn't always sure whether the images he recalled were genuine or imagined. The mind, he suspected, wasn't designed to store so much data.

What if I were to tell my own story? Where would it begin? With a joke, of course. Even my dreams were jokes, gags inserted in the midst of a film noir that was, of late, plunging into steeper horrors. But maybe Borges would tire of me eventually and let me die. Even if he didn't, I'd know Lenny was out there somewhere because I'd stood up and said no, I wouldn't sacrifice him.

"Tell me more about your father," I said.

"First, tell me about your mother."

"She's still a puzzle. But now I know she loved me, and I can remember her face." I tried not to look for signs of Isaac as I looked at Lenny.

"That voice. The one that spoke to my father, it never spoke to me. Now I think . . . it was the voice of The Beast. You call him Borges. Ruth, I know you're scared." He kissed my head like I was a child. "But it's going to be all right. Really. Better than you think."

I reached out to hold his hand and squeezed too tightly. "We don't know who he is, do we? Borges?"

He nodded.

"Maybe your father didn't know either. Not for sure. Maybe he acted out of hope. . . . You think I'm a fool, don't you?" He didn't disagree. "Look, if it was the devil who spoke to your father, wouldn't the devil have let him kill you?"

"And God wouldn't?"

"I don't know. But whatever we think we know, we're just guessing, like everyone else, and even if we guess right, Borges won't tell us."

"You're assuming he has the answers."

"I know *I* don't. And I doubt your father did either. But you still resent him, don't you?"

"I don't think so. Not anymore."

"Have you ever wondered—" He looked so hopeful. I adored him so.

"Say it," he said gently.

"The way we feel about each other—whether it's just as false and deliberate as the way we met? Because he arranged that, you know, Borges."

"So maybe he arranges everything?"

"Or whoever controls him."

He tilted his head. Big grin. "Not for a moment would I ever believe that."

"Why not?"

"Because even if we *were* actors in somebody's play—and we're not—we have to live our lives as though we control them. Otherwise, what's the point?"

"You've got that part sorted out, don't you?"

"I've had time to think about it."

I hugged him and held on.

"You're right," I said. "Maybe—maybe he envies what we have together, whoever he is."

"Exactly."

"And he *wants* us to feel helpless."

"But we're not," he said.

"You're right, you're so right."

"But the trouble is—"

"What" I asked him.

"Well, look around. Justice? Where's the justice?"

"We're here together. Isn't that justice?"

LENNY

She was right. Not everything is ugly. Some people even die happy, contented. I'd seen it, seen beauty, serenity, unselfish love. I'd seen people revitalized through prayer, just as The Beast said, even if he did laugh at them. I'm pretty sure some of those people didn't believe any God was listening, but it helped them anyway. When you know a placebo is a placebo and it still works, that's one powerful placebo. None of that was the devil's work. Neither was Ruth.

So many mornings I'd opened my eyes in the dreamy twilight between sleep and wakefulness, not fully understanding my location or the circumstances around me, but still eager for the day to begin. That wasn't the devil's work either.

"Lenny—should I still call you Lenny?" I nodded. "What did Borges say to you?" She watched me carefully, the perfect woman, according to him. Well, he'd have her no more.

I tried to explain how much it meant to me to converse with The Beast at last, despite the mystery of him remaining largely unsolved. Of course that didn't answer her question. She took another tack: "How could you have waited so long to tell someone about yourself? When I think about it, it doesn't seem possible."

"I told you. I'm not supposed to."

"That doesn't make sense. Who says you're not supposed to?"

"I don't know, but I know I'm not a prophet. I might not even be so unique. Maybe others out there could tell stories like mine. Millions even. Maybe The Beast isn't so unique either. Maybe there are other inscrutable beings who go around keeping track of the ones like me. There were—"

"What?"

"People—not many—who knew about me. Something anyway. They sensed it."

"What kind of people?"

"I don't know what you mean."

"Well, for starters, were they men people or women people?"

"Women," I said.

"Always women."

"I think so, yes."

She studied me a moment. "How many women have you stayed with? Fifty? A thousand? Ten thousand?"

"It was mostly one at a time."

"Do you remember their names?"

"Some of them."

"Will you remember mine?"

"That's partly up to you, isn't it? Try to be memorable."

"Don't joke. Precisely how did it end? These women you stayed with?"

"Some went a little crazy. So I got in the habit of getting away early. That's why I said goodbye to you."

"But you didn't say goodbye. You just ran off." Her voice and expressions were different now, harder, flatter. She was moving toward the outcome I had to have, but I didn't understand why.

"Lenny, do you believe I love you?"

"Yes."

"Good. Then ditch the contraption around your ankle and take off. Please."

"I might if you quit the Arthur Trianon Institute." A quick vision of the name on a door flashed before me, and I was queasy for a moment. It was part of the unreachable memory of that night. "Ruth, you have to get away from Borges. And I'll disappear, just as you said. Now's your chance."

She looked pained, suddenly. I supposed she sensed a lie. I wasn't made for this. I reached over to kiss her again, but something stopped me. When I pulled back, she was looking at me like a waif suddenly face to face with being left alone. "I can't just quit. I have a career."

RUTH

"I *don't* have to get away. I don't *want* to. We've had our goodbye now, Lenny. It's all I wanted. I'll never forget you, but it's time. It really is."

He bent his head, lost in thought, exasperation, or both, then spoke slowly. "I don't want to stay with you either. I never did. I never said I did. What I'm trying to explain is that you don't need him. Don't you understand that? You don't need him *or* me. You can be free."

"I don't like hurting you, Lenny, but what I have now is everything. How many people walk away from everything?"

"You talk like a slave."

I couldn't keep this up any longer. I slapped him with the back of my hand, cutting his cheek with a ring that once belonged to Evelyn's mother. For a mini-moment I was ready to confess everything and beg forgiveness, but he slapped me back hard and quick, his hand like a lunging snake. I tasted blood, and his face looked crazy, not like Lenny at all. "I can't let you stay with him," he said. He placed his powerful hands on my throat.

"God help you," I said.

He laughed a crazy kind of short, hard laugh, mumbled something in another language, and said, "That's the stupidest fucking thing I ever heard."

"Do it," I said. He shut his eyes. I shut mine. He exhaled an awful whoosh of despair, an animal sound, and then dropped his hands. As I opened my eyes he was dressing in a frenzy. He fled with his shoes in his hand. It was, after all, what I'd asked him to do. It seemed so very quiet. Wrapped in the dreadful bedspread, I stood up and looked down ten stories through the streaked window. I could barely see New Jersey across the haze that clung to the river. I wondered how that river looked four thousand years ago.

Somehow, after all we'd endured to be together, we'd pried ourselves apart as easily as bark off a dead branch.

I don't know how much time passed. The window represented weakness. Maybe it's what Borges wanted from me all along, wanted me to see it on my own, though I wasn't sure it would even work. And I *am* weak. Everything was just too hard, one awful puzzle leading to the next. I wasn't brave enough to stay with Borges, but I couldn't bear to know Lenny was suffering, so I'd do what's easy, or at least try to. If Lenny were to suffer anyway, then maybe I wouldn't know about it. Maybe I could shut off everything, including the dreams. I couldn't bear Borges in my dreams.

The old, wooden window was stuck, probably painted shut. I looked around for something to break it with. And the door opened.

"Can't get the window open?" Lenny said. He was panting. He'd been running. I stood mute. "Well, get your own window. I'm jumping out of this one."

I searched his eyes, his beautiful black eyes. "Try it," I said, "and I'll kill you."

He nodded toward the rainy streets below. "What good would it do anyway?"

"That's what I've been trying to figure out," I said. "We both made the same bargain, didn't we?"

He took me in his arms. "That's right, genius."

"So now what do we do?"

"I don't know, but whatever it is, why not do it together?"

"Whither thou goest," I said, "I will go."

I waited my whole life to say that.

CHAPTER 21

BORGES

One of them turning me down I could almost understand. But both of them? The possibility never occurred to me. When I got over being offended, I was, to my surprise, amused. Beware of those good deeds. The repercussions can lead you places you never thought you'd have to go.

And now they'd come looking for answers. Everyone wants answers, everyone wants justice. When they're not complaining about God or fate, they complain about each other. No one seems to meet their expectations, and when something makes them happy, they quickly grow tired of it and complain some more. Sometimes in groups. *You're not going to leave us here like this, are you?* Those who cry the loudest are often the least deserving of all.

What if I said everything is designed to work precisely the way it does work for as long as it's supposed to work? *Everything? What about the typhus microbe that killed Anne Frank at Bergen-Belsen? That too?* You bet. You know something? Most people would find such an answer comforting. *Ah, there really is a hand on the tiller.* Because their greatest fear is uncertainty. Sentence a man to twenty years without parole and he might emerge highly functional. Give the same man an indeterminate sentence, kick him loose in five years, and he'll be a ruined human being. Folks want to *know*, and they want it all served in a precisely balanced metaphysical nectar. Of course there are always the ones that peer into tangles of contradiction and ambiguity and see what they think is clarity. Well let them see it then, but an indeterminate sentence is all they get.

LENNY

One invention I've never learned to embrace is the telephone—a sorry instrument of blind communication. This time, however, I was delighted to answer it.

"Dr. Borges would like to meet with you," said the voice.

RUTH

Lenny hung up and said, "He wants to see us." We studied the concrete beneath the window—so bereft of irony or subtlety.

"Do you think," I asked him, "that's what he wanted us to do?"

"Maybe. Maybe he still wants it."

We found Borges getting what appeared to be a pedicure and foot massage in a Fifth Avenue salon. Like his hotel in Santa Monica, the place was too upscale to put out a sign. After getting past a doorman with a barely discernible instrument in his ear, we were confronted by a tall brunette who reeked of contempt. Emitting a faint trail of exquisite perfume, she led us to Borges and left without a word. He was reclining like a barefoot pasha in a private booth as big as a boxcar. He dismissed his foot attendants with a wave of the long fingers that poked out of his bandage.

"Borges, you told me you never lie to me," I said. "But the stories you told us don't match."

"I see why you like this one, Yitzhak. She's a keeper."

Don't fall for his tricks, I reminded myself, and then I reminded Lenny.

BORGES

Flush with impudence, they took turns scolding me. Part of the time they even ignored my presence, speaking back and forth as though I were a poodle who just happened to be in the room. But eventually they began plying me with questions, typical questions for the most part, though I can't be sure because I didn't listen all that carefully. *Who are you?* of course. That was to be expected. And, *Why did this happen? Or that?* Why did it *not* happen? They wondered about the precise role of chaos. *Is it part of the plan? And if it is, why does it have to be so chaotic?* Not to mention cause and effect, justice and injustice. The usual. Did they ever stop to think how blessed they were to have the capacity to form these questions? If a beast is sinking in a bog, it doesn't wonder why it's there or blame itself or anyone else, or think back step by step to what led it there. It just tries to get out. I wonder how many people would prefer to live as beasts. Possibly most of them.

To their credit, these two never asked about life after death. In fact, they refrained from crystal ball questions altogether. I let them wear themselves down and finally asked them who gave them their names. They answered impatiently, as though *I* were taking up *their* valuable time. Imagine, I told this troublesome team of two, you're in an endless void, with no one there to name you, no one to tell you who you are or how long you've been there. You just *are*. With no one to invent the very concept of a name. No one to tell you anything at all.

"You know who you are," one of them said. No respect at all. Yet they expected *me* to feel compassion for *them*. Each in turn groused about their little bumps and bruises though both had been *polished* by abuse while being spared all manner of more wretched possibilities. The mysteries that confound them bring them discomfort only because they lack fundamental understanding. So they accuse.

"But why do we lack understanding?"

It never ends. I knew I deserved their complaints, but not for the reasons they assumed. I deserved them for granting them an extra measure of kindness, particularly to Yitzhak, who never had to worry about those little aches and pains in the night that might signal cancer, meningitis, or other unpleasantries he needn't concern himself with.

Even though I'd lost my bets on both of them I remained amused. And yes, looked at from their perspective I'd failed to keep my word—a complaint that gets my attention. I'd been tricked at my own game, unable to punish one without breaking my bargain with the other; but I solved that, at least for now, because over time they'll learn that Ruth now possesses the same gift as Yitzhak. In this way I kept my word to both of them.

They don't bore me. I'll give them that. You should *see* some of the ones I have to deal with. "If you expect us to worship you," Ruth said on the way out, "forget it." I shook my head, betraying nothing.